# Angel Of The Evening

*by*

Rowena Summers

**Magna Large Print Books**
Long Preston, North Yorkshire,
England.

British Library Cataloguing in Publication Data.



Summers, Rowena
Angel of the evening.

A catalogue record for this book is available from the British Library

ISBN 0-7505-0538-9

First published in Great Britain by Severn House Publishers Ltd., 1992



Published in Large Print 1993 by arrangement with Severn House Publishers Ltd.



Magna Large Print is an imprint of
Library Magna Books Ltd.
Printed and bound in Great Britain by
T.J. Press (Padstow) Ltd., Cornwall, PL28 8RW.

# CHAPTER 1

Brie was beginning to feel slightly disorientated. She had lost sight of her room-mate Claire, a long while back. Surrounded now by the weirdest characters she had ever seen in her life, she was nearly deafened by the babble going on all around her. It bordered on the hysterical, and added to that, the champagne was going to her head.

A science fiction convention, for heaven's sake! It wasn't her thing at all, and never had been, even if Claire was addicted to all the sci-fi books and films she could find. If she hadn't found it all so unbelievable, Brie might be totally unnerved by now, and resentful of Claire's apparent desertion. This whole attendance had been Claire's idea, of course.

'Say you'll come, Brie. It'll be the experience of a lifetime,' Claire had almost begged, excitement making her square features prettier than usual. 'The last one was a riot! Authors and readers wearing the most fantastic costumes to illustrate characters from the books, and some of them were incredibly imaginative—'

'I saw the photos, remember?' Brie had said with a grin, unable to imagine the kind of people so eager to dress up as robots and spacemen and plant-people for an entire weekend. It was a kind of exhibitionism she couldn't understand. She was miles more extrovert than Claire, who would doubtless appear at the convention as her natural, sensible self, but even Brie drew the line at this kind of circus.

'Please, Brie. We won't have much longer to enjoy each other's company. You'll be going off on this new job at the end of next week, and with any luck my transfer to the York branch will have come through before you get back.'

She held up crossed fingers as she spoke, her pale eyes shining behind the owl-glasses. Claire was a librarian, and with her love of books, she always said the County should be paid by her for the privilege of working there, instead of the other way round. Brie was still reluctant about going to the convention on the South coast with her, when Claire played her trump card.

'Your Adam Andrikos will be there, Brie. Looking for likely scripts for a new TV series, apparently.'

She had definitely caught Brie's attention now.

'He's hardly *my* Adam Andrikos! I haven't even seen the man yet!' And she was still disturbed, resentful, curious, about a man who could hire someone the way he had hired her, without even meeting her. Yes, her references had been impeccable, and evidently that had been enough. Brie felt her soft mouth tighten, wondering what kind of man could hand over his young sister to a stranger's care so unconcernedly.

She had focused her blue eyes more keenly on Claire then, and as always her friend sighed with envy at the brilliant clarity of that look. They were complete opposites in looks and character, yet they had formed a close friendship in the rooming house. Claire would never rival Brie's delicate, fragile appearance that hid a strong and determined will, and frequently moaned in mock despair as she tried to tame her own brown locks to resemble Brie's long cornsilk hair...

'How do you know Adam Andrikos will

be there?' Brie demanded to know.

'Don't you ever read the newspapers? This convention hasn't exactly gone unnoticed by the media, Brie! Here, take a look while I have a shower.'

She handed Brie a newspaper folded open at the entertainment page, on her way to the bathroom. Brie found herself reading it with an almost avid interest, despite herself. Adam Andrikos was not her favourite man of the moment. She was quite ready to despise him, and was filled with pity for the young schoolgirl sister, daughter of his father's second wife, who was so ruthlessly delegated to a stranger's care.

Yes, he would be at the convention, the interview announced. And he would be scouting for a new sci-fi series to produce for TV, just as Claire had said. One more success to add to his string of successes...and there was his photo, smiling out of the newsprint with more than a hint of impatience in the smile, as Brie would have expected from him.

Ever since she had been interviewed by his PR person, vetted and passed after rigorous enquiries as to her suitability for the job, she had had the feeling that she was about to be in the employ of an automaton, a machine. No wonder Adam Andrikos' sci-fi series were so excellent in their slick perfection. He was more robot than man himself. He had no heart.

Brie's own heart gave a sudden leap as she studied the handsome dark face in the newspaper. She hadn't seen a picture of him before. He was very dark, as she'd have expected from his Greek heritage. He was only half-Greek, with accounted for his English-sounding first name, and that of his sister, Susan. The senior Andrikos had married two English women, and Adam and Susan had resulted.

Adam Andrikos had dark eyes beneath the brooding heavy brows, and a hawklike nose, very strong and straight. He had high foreign cheekbones, and his mouth—his mouth seemed to be stretched wide in the forced smile for the camera. Brie guessed instantly that he wasn't a man who suffered fools gladly, and would find a photo call for a tabloid newspaper both an intrusion and time-wasting. It was a shrewd assessment of the man, but Brie had a knack of getting instant assessments right.

So this was Adam Andrikos. She

admitted that she was mildly surprised. She had expected the dynamic tycoon, but she hadn't expected him to be quite so good-looking, so sexy...nor only 35 years old, as the paper stated. You had few secrets once you were in the public's eye...

For a brief moment, Brie wondered how it must feel to live in such a goldfish bowl of publicity. How would *she* feel? How would they report *her* in the usual journalese jargon? She found herself composing an imaginary piece of copy, adding her own statistics to the requirements of the new job.

'Petite, honey-blonde Brie Roberts, aged 23, was hired by TV tycoon Adam Andrikos to escort his sister Susan Andrikos to the family home in Corfu. Miss Roberts' qualifications for the post consisted of a two-year child-care course, and a further three years as nanny to Lady Finola Beale-Underwood's young children. Miss Roberts was hired as much for her obvious ability to deal with children as for her own youthful appearance, which it is hoped will aid her in her task with the reputedly wilful and precocious Miss Susan Andrikos.'

Brie smiled ruefully at that point. The

PR person had left her in no doubt that a month in the company of Susan Andrikos was a challenge in itself. The girl was still away at boarding-school for the moment. She was nearly fourteen years old, but according to Miss Lacey, the PR person, she was the most adult thirteen-year-old of the century, and one that the high-priced boarding-school would be glad to see the back of for the long summer holidays. Adam himself intended going to Corfu in a month's time, when Brie would be released. Miss Lacey had made it sound a little like a jail sentence.

All the same, Brie was a born optimist, and she hoped that she and Susan would be friends. Added to which, the thought of spending a blissful month on the lovely verdant island of Corfu was too inviting to resist. After the gloom of an English winter and the cold damp spring, Corfu beckoned like an oasis in the desert.

And now the piquancy of seeing Adam Andrikos at close quarters at this sci-fi convention at Bournemouth, the week before she was due to meet Susan at Luton airport for the flight, had also proved irresistible. So here she was, crushed on all sides by moon-men, clanking, mechanical beings and gory-looking beasts, each more spectacular than the last, and no sign of a familiar face anywhere. Not Claire's. Not Adam Andrikos'.

It was the evening cocktail party before the first-night dinner, and no doubt Claire was rushing about collecting autographs, or drooling in a corner somewhere with a favourite author or set of bookish characters, and in her seventh heaven.

While Brie had yet to track down Adam Andrikos, if he even deigned to appear, she thought suspiciously. The media often got it wrong, and press releases weren't always to be trusted. She may have come here for nothing. She wasn't exactly sure what she would do when she did see him. She didn't intend presenting herself to him!

She wondered if he too would be done up in some outlandish gear. Was he that type of man? Somehow Brie didn't think so, but how could she tell? What type was he? He must have some good points about him, but Brie still thought him heartless to send his sister home in a stranger's care. The girl's parents—Adam's father and stepmother—had died six months ago, and this would be the first time Susan had gone home since then. Surely he could have spared some of his precious time to go with her!

Brie felt her arm shoved aside by a green-scaled monster, and her wine slopped over the middle of her silky blue cocktail dress. The monster turned clumsily to apologise, so awkward in his costume that he bumped her again.

'It's perfectly all right,' Brie muttered, thinking how much this dress had cost. Adam was paying her very well for the month, and she had been reckless in stocking up with new clothes more suited to the hot dry Greek climate. This cocktail dress was one of them, and she didn't want it ruined before she even reached Corfu.

Glancing down, she felt acutely embarrassed at seeing the transparent patch over her midriff now, where the champagne had slopped. The green-scaled monster was still apologising behind his gruesome mask.

'Look, I have to join my Terror Lagoon group now, but I'll look out for you later, and buy you another drink, if I may, Miss—Miss—'

'It's really not necessary—'

'It will be my pleasure, and it would make me feel much better, honestly— '

'Meanwhile,' said a deeper, more authoritative voice right behind Brie's head, 'I'll take care of the young lady. I believe your Terror Lagoon group is gathering in the sun lounge.'

Brie hardly saw the monster leave. Even before she turned round, a sixth sense told her whose voice it would be. Her heart beat more erratically, more loudly, as her eyes met the dark, brooding gaze of Adam Andrikos. His piercing eyes were almost black as they seemed to lock with Brie's. She had to tilt her head to look up at him, so perfectly-dressed in comparison with the garish outfits of the sci-fi fanatics.

As if to scorn the genre that had made him famous with his T.V. productions, he wore an expensively-cut black evening suit and bow tie, with a dazzling white frilled shirt beneath. With his teak-swarthy complexion and glossy black hair curling slightly into his nape, he was even more of a man than his newspaper photo could ever portray. He was the epitome of dark sexual masculinity.

He couldn't know her identity, and yet she had the oddest feeling that he knew exactly who she was. As though he could see right through her reason for being here as easily as he could see through the flimsy fabric clinging to her midriff rather uncomfortably now. She had only intended to view him from afar, to observe, not to be thrust into his company.

Nor to feel the sudden awareness of the way his gaze had begun a slow, insolent appraisal of her, from the top of her head, where she had piled her fine-spun hair in silken swathes to give her some height for the evening, down over her flushed features, her slender shoulders and gently curving shape, to the high-heeled silver sandals. And back again, to where the dampness of the wine revealed the flesh-coloured midriff beneath the blue dress...

'You'd better sponge that off,' he said abruptly. 'I doubt that it will stain, but I'd prefer not to have a dinner partner reeking of wine. A few minutes near the hand drier in the Ladies Room will soon dry you off. I'll wait for you here.'

Brie's mouth fell open as he took the wine glass from her hand. Dinner partner? She had no intention of being Adam Andrikos' dinner partner! She could never keep up the charade. It would be ridiculous to try. When he came to Corfu in a month's time and found out who she was, he would think she had been practising some kind of personal deception for her own purposes. Maybe he'd think she was an aspiring TV actress, which couldn't be farther from the truth. She had better tell him right now that she'd be sitting with a friend for dinner...

He had moved away and been claimed by a screaming group of foil-clad ladies before Brie got a chance to say a word. What characters they were meant to depict, she couldn't imagine. While she was still furious at herself for standing there so dumbly while Adam Andrikos had taken command of her, Claire came rushing up, her eyes shining.

'I've been looking for you everywhere. Why are you all wet? Oh, never mind. I've met the most fabulous author. He writes as Diablo Hades, get it? His real name's Bill Jones.' She giggled, obviously awash with champagne and high on excitement at meeting her idols. 'Come to the Ladies Room with me a minute, Brie. I'm sitting with Bill for dinner. You don't mind, do you? You can scrub yourself dry while we talk. How did you get so wet, anyway?'

She rattled on without ever waiting for any answers. It seemed to settle the question of whether Claire wanted her company at dinner, anyway. She naturally assumed that Brie would find her own company. Brie was normally so much more self-assured than Claire that she could hardly begrudge her this night of excitement, nor her meeting with Bill/Diablo, whoever he was...Brie felt the laughter bubbling up in her own throat. It was infectious, and she was beginning to feel reckless.

So she was going to be stuck with Adam Andrikos for dinner. It wasn't any of her doing, and if he thought it was a put-up-job, then the sooner she told him it wasn't, the better for their relationship. Brief though it might be, she didn't want to antagonise her temporary boss. She'd tell him the minute she had dried off her dress—always supposing he really was still waiting for her. With his looks and the way every other female was eyeing him earlier, he would probably have got way-laid long ago. Well, it would be a relief if it happened, even if it meant she was on her own for dinner.

The bursts of laughter all around her made her smile. No-one was alone at a convention like this, but you could still feel lonely when everyone else was part of a group or a couple. And she wasn't going to tag along with Claire and her new-found friend who could put such a glow on Claire's pale cheeks, either.

She sponged her dress and dried it dutifully under the hand drier, trying not to remember that she was following Adam's instructions. He definitely had an air of authority about him, she thought again. When he spoke, everybody jumped. When he commanded, everybody obeyed. No wonder he got such a good response from the people who worked under him, if all that the critics said was true.

The heat of the drier on her stomach was getting to be too much, and anyway, the flimsy material had dried very quickly. Claire was ready, having applied more lipstick than usual, her eyes outlined now in sparkly gold. Obviously the flamboyance of the company was even getting to Claire. Unless it was all due to the unknown Bill/Diablo, of course...

'I'll see you later then, Brie. Have a good time—and don't do anything I wouldn't do!' Claire giggled again.

It wasn't the kind of remark she usually made, and Brie watched her move away and get swallowed up by the crowd. She smiled affectionately. At least this weekend was bringing Claire out of her shell, which couldn't be bad. It might even change her life, if Bill/Diablo turned out to be Mr Right...

She must stop thinking in clichés, Brie told herself crossly, suddenly aware of the fact that she was standing there smiling inanely at nothing in particular. And then her vision was blocked by a dark shape right in front of her, and Adam Andrikos was holding out his arm to her. It would have been churlish not to take it, and Brie found her arm held fast by his powerful clasp as he wound his way in and out of the crush of people, making sure she didn't escape.

The dining-hall seemed to be bursting with colour when they entered. Those who weren't in costume glittered just from being there, and flash-bulbs seemed to be popping everywhere as press and personal cameras recorded the scene. T.V. cameras trailed around the tables, and felt-covered boom mikes hovered over anyone who looked interesting enough to be interviewed.

Adam found them two places to sit.

Seating was informal, and as soon as they were settled, Brie looked at him with sudden nervousness. Once he knew her name, maybe he'd be angry with her, but since she hated deception and believed in saying what was on her mind straight away, she took a deep breath.

'I think we should introduce ourselves. I already know—'

His large hand covered hers on the white tablecloth. The fingers were strong, curling around Brie's. They were tanned, as though he spent a long time outdoors in healthy pursuits, the nails clipped to a businesslike length. She liked his hands, the thought flashed through her mind.

'I don't think we should,' he was smiling at her, and the smile was vastly different from the arrogant, impatient one he had used for the newspaper picture she had seen. This smile was wide, sexy, intimate. It was a smile that had the instant effect of making Brie feel as though her toes were curling. A very private smile in a very public room. He went on speaking, his voice low and intimate too. She could imagine it raised in anger, but its timbre now was seductively warm. Brie felt a sudden shiver run through her.

'Why should we two ruin the effect of the night, when these people have gone to so much trouble to make themselves look so spectacular? Let's go along with their mood. For all you know, I could be the devil in disguise, and you—now, what and who are you, I wonder?'

His smile teased her as he studied her face, flushed with the scrutiny, and more than that. She felt as though every pore was exposed to his gaze as he took in the softness of her skin, and the way her lashes fringed her cornflower blue eyes. Hers was a very English beauty, and she had never felt more conscious of her own delicate colouring compared with his. Dark against light...power against fragility...

'I'll call you angel for the evening,' he went on. 'The angel and the devil—how about that?'

'Is that what you want?' Brie knew she was taking the coward's way out at that moment, prolonging the charade, and yet in those tingling moments when the warm pressure of Adam's fingers caressed hers ever so gently, she knew she didn't want to see the contemptuous look come into his eyes just yet, when he discovered that she was Brie Roberts. Just for an hour or so, she would be his angel of the evening...

She swallowed as he nodded, his head leaning towards hers in a conspiratorial way.

'Why not? I rather like a woman of mystery, and I'd far rather see you without some of the trappings these others have disguised themselves with. At least you don't disguise the fact that you're a real woman!'

His eyes followed the line of the blue dress, where it hugged the contours of her breasts. The neckline was low, and in it Brie wore a silver filigree necklace. She was uncomfortably aware that Adam Andrikos noted the way it rose and fell on the creamy skin as she responded to that look. He was a very sensual man, a type she had seen often when she had worked with Lady Finola's children. They had come to the stately home in droves at weekends, and had thought the children's nanny an added bonus among the debby young women who were house-guests. They had soon learned that Brie Roberts wasn't there as weekend sport. Any more than she was now.

'A real woman with a mind and will of her own,' she said sweetly now to Adam. 'Don't let the air of helplessness fool you. Even angels can be temperamental if provoked.'

He laughed, a rich sexy sound. 'Good. I don't like my women to be docile. And the devil in me relates to that sparkle in your eyes. Do you know that you have the most beautiful blue eyes I've ever seen?'

He threw the compliment at her so suddenly it took her by surprise. She blushed, and then blinked as a flash-bulb went off in front of her. Next minute, the T.V. cameraman had neared their table, and Adam smiled ruefully.

'My cover is about to be blown,' he commented. 'I didn't think I'd get away with it for long.'

The mike was held in front of him, and at once he became the tycoon producer, used to speaking publicly in succinct phrases and saying just what he wanted to and no more. Introduced by an eager interviewer as the famed and successful Adam Andrikos, Brie could only admire his composure and technique. They knew immediately when Adam had said all he intended to say, and she felt a sudden horror as the cameraman swung his camera towards her.

'May we ask the name of your charming

companion, Mr Andrikos?' the suave interviewer said.

Brie's mouth went dry. Adam may be used to TV interviews, but she was not. She felt him cover her hand with his own again, and heard his easy laugh.

'We're all meant to be here incognito at this convention, and I'm not sure I want to share my angel of the evening with you all. However, since you'll find out anyway, my friend is Miss Brie Roberts, and she'll be flying out to my home in Corfu next week to accompany my sister there.'

# CHAPTER 2

When the TV people had moved on, Brie turned on Adam in a fury, snatching her hand away from his.

'You knew all along who I was,' she raged.

'And you knew who I was,' he said calmly.

'I never tried to deny that. I wanted to tell you when we sat down, if you remember. You were the one who wanted to keep up the mystery, not me! And what kind of interpretation do you think those TV people will put on what you just said? They'll have a field-day now, and so will the newspapers. They'll think we're having an affair or something. You know how they gossip if you give them the slightest chance—'

He let her storm on, sitting there with a complacent smile on his face. Brie wanted to hit him. How could he be so thoughtless? If it *was* thoughtless. His words had taken her completely by surprise.

She wouldn't have thought Adam Andrikos a man who encouraged the kind of gutter gossip some of the newspapers employed. Neither would she have thought him a man who gave such information away so carelessly. He seemed too much in control of any situation for that.

'Would it bother you—to let them think we were having an affair? You don't strike me as a Victorian governess-type, for all that your references from Lady Finola double-barelled surname were so impressive!'

Of course, he would know all about her. Her details weren't confined solely to the PR person, then. She was glad to know that much, but right now it was the least of her problems.

'Yes, it would bother me!' She almost hissed, aware that other people were joining them at their table. 'I've no wish to get that kind of publicity, thank you very much.'

'Good. I'm glad to hear it's only the publicity angle you're worried about,' Adam retorted, turning away from her a moment to greet some people he knew. Though how he recognised them, Brie couldn't guess. They seemed to be covered from head to toe in shiny gold paint. They looked as if they had been poured into their skin-fitting costumes. Across the table the green-scaled monster raised his champagne glass to her, and Brie tried to give him a smile back that wasn't a grimace. She felt shaken by Adam's stupid remarks, and was only just beginning to realise what he had just said.

Did it mean he wouldn't be averse to having an affair with her? Was that what he expected from every attractive young woman he hired? Brie felt a brief disappointment. If it wasn't for his high-powered image, she might even have liked him. Now, with everything he said to her, she was finding less and less to like in him. And if he thought she was some little star-struck girl who was ready to fall into bed with him at the first opportunity, then he could think again!

In those sporting weekends at Lady Finola's, there had been eager young Lords and the occasional Duke who had thought the same thing. She hadn't fallen for them, and she wasn't falling for any line that T.V tycoon Adam Andrikos could hand out. Brie's eyes suddenly sparkled. With any luck, she would be his first failure. She hoped so. She hoped so very much.

He turned back to her, and Brie smiled into his eyes, glad that he couldn't read her mind just then. Maybe she should give him a run for his money, and then let him know that there were still girls left in the world to whom falling in love was something special. Still some girls who didn't tumble in and out of bed with any man who asked them, but preferred to wait for one very important man in their lives. Brie was a girl who believed in love, passionately and unreservedly, and when that man came along, she blissfully expected to share the rest of her life with him. If it was romantic and idealistic, then she was both a romantic and an idealist and admitted it.

'I presume your Miss Lacey described me to you,' she said, remembering the vetting she had gone through in the woman's office. 'I had assumed you didn't much care who escorted your sister home.'

'Then you assumed wrong.' Brie saw at once that she had caught him on a nerve. 'My sister is not the easiest of young girls, and I had to be sure I had hired the right person. Not only did I read your dossier, but you remember you sent a photo to Miss Lacey as well.'

No, Brie hadn't remembered until this minute! How stupid of her to forget. But then, she hadn't expected Adam Andrikos to have concerned himself with her file. But that meant he had known who she was all the time. From the minute he'd seen the wine spilt on her dress he had marked her out. It hadn't been any idle pick-up that made him want her for his dinner partner. He'd clearly wondered how far she would go before admitting who she was. Naturally with his ego, he'd assume that she knew exactly who he was!

Well, now they could stop pretending with one another.

'I'm perfectly sure I can cope with Susan,' Brie said coolly, on her home ground now. 'I'm trained in dealing with difficult children—'

Adam laughed grimly. 'The first thing you'll discover, my sweet angel, is that Susan is not a child. She's the most irritating, awkward, difficult and aggressive young girl it's been my misfortune to know, and that comes from someone fond of her!'

'Really?' Brie bristled at his patronising tone, filled with renewed pity for Susan Andrikos, despite his description of her, which was obviously biased. 'You could have fooled me. It sounded like someone who disliked her intensely.'

'You're speaking solely as an Englishwoman, angel. I have the advantage of having Greek blood in my veins as well as the more reserved English variety, as does Susan. Love and hate run very closely together in any relationship, and the fact that we shout and scream at each other and recognise our bad traits, as well as our good, does not mean we care any the less for one another! I merely want to warn you that if you start treating Susan as one of your meek and mild English aristocracy, you'll be in for a rude awakening. And I would hate to see such a beautiful angel trampled on.'

Brie looked at him coldly. Under cover of the table conversation and the waiters serving the meal now, Adam managed to keep up the conversation between the two of them alone. And Brie was chagrined to notice that people were beginning to take an interest in the way the two of them seemed so intent on each other. The T.V interview had probably begun it, but now she noticed people with Press badges on their lapels hovering near. The last thing

Brie wanted was for the media to suspect a romantic link between them. Apart from being totally false, it could hardly do her relationship with Susan Andrikos any good if the girl was going to be as difficult as Adam intimated.

'Could we postpone this discussion until some other time, please?' she asked him. 'People are becoming too interested in us.'

'Certainly.' He gave all his attention from then on to one of the gold-skinned ladies, and it was so obvious, after Brie's aside to him, she guessed that any media people who were interested in them would see it as deliberate to divert their own attention. Probably they weren't at all interested, Brie thought hopefully. And then realised that it was unlikely they would come down here to cover this convention unless they were very much interested. And a juicy little tit-bit of gossip regarding one of their top TV producers was always good for copy. She hated Adam for amusing himself in this way. He might find it intriguing to fool the Press, but Brie wasn't used to such ways, and didn't like them one bit. She believed in honesty and integrity, and to her mind, Adam Andrikos had displayed little of either in any of his dealings with her so far.

She was thankful when the meal was over and guests began to mingle. There were author signing sessions in one of the lounges, and Claire rushed up to her, saying that her Bill was about to be in the limelight. Already he was 'her Bill', Brie noted. When Claire pointed out the man dressed in devil's gear, complete with silver cape and red horns, she thought fleetingly that this should be Adam's garb, not Bill Jones', alias Diablo Hades. But Bill was having his moments of glory, surrounded by his fans, and she could see that Claire was enjoying every vicarious minute of his success.

'Bill lives in Leeds,' she said, amazement in her voice. 'When I move to York with the transfer, we'll only be a few miles from each other.'

It was obviously fate, and from the way Bill's eyes kept straying from the mound of books he was signing for his fans, he evidently saw Claire as his kismet too.

'Did I see you with Adam Andrikos, Brie? He's pretty dishy, isn't he? Did you introduce yourself to him? I knew you'd be glad you came to the convention.'

'Don't you ever stop for breath?' Brie asked her. 'Yes, I was with him. Yes, he's dishy. No, I didn't introduce myself to him, since he knew who I was from my photo. And I'm not sure if I'm glad I'm here or not.'

'Oh!' Claire was stopped in her tracks at all that. 'We'll have to make sure you enjoy it then, won't we? Bill's asked me to some club he knows down here tomorrow night. If you'd like to join us, you're welcome, Brie. Or maybe I shouldn't have accepted. After all, we did come here together—'

She looked so down for a second that Brie burst out laughing. Her feelings were plain on her face. Claire didn't have many men-friends, and it was so obvious that she and Bill had hit it off from the minute they met that the wonder of it shone out of her. Not for worlds would Brie spoil things for her. She gave her a quick hug.

'I have plans of my own for tomorrow night,' she lied.

'Good. I hope they include Adam whatsit,' Claire said happily. 'You two looked really good together, Brie. Everybody on my table was saying so.'

'Claire—' Brie said in exasperation. Her

room-mate was forever saying she didn't understand why Brie hadn't married some well-heeled Lord ages ago, with all her connections at Lady Finola's, and since she hadn't done so, seemed hell-bent on finding a suitable husband for her. Brie's warning exclamation was usually enough to make Claire back off, but tonight she was as high as if she had drunk a bottle of champagne to herself.

'All right, all right,' Claire laughed. 'But you're not going to stop people speculating. A.A's just about the most eligible man around here, and you know how the Press scents a romance—'

'There isn't any romance, for heaven's sake!' Brie hissed at her. 'And you just make sure you don't go hinting that there is, all right?'

She couldn't diminish Claire's glow tonight, and she wouldn't want to. Just as long as nobody started pairing herself off with Adam Andrikos! Brie felt an odd little thrill run through her at the thought, and decided it was mainly nerves at just what the Press might make of it tomorrow.

'Are you coming into the dance, Brie? It's starting soon.'

'No thanks. I don't fancy being clasped to some green monster's chest,' Brie grinned at her. 'You go and enjoy yourself with Bill. I'm going for a walk along the cliffs to get some fresh air, and then I'll probably go to bed. And stop looking so worried! Go and enjoy yourself. You don't have to nursemaid me, just because all this was your idea!'

'You aren't sorry, are you?' Claire was reluctant to leave her, torn between guilt and her obvious longing to get back to Bill, and Brie laughed, her eyes dancing.

'Are you kidding? I wouldn't have missed it for anything.' She was surprised to find that it was true. 'Even meeting Adam Andrikos had to happen sooner or later, and it's been—well, interesting, if nothing else. I'm even curious to hear his talk at tomorrow's seminar, though how they can all take this sci-fi stuff so seriously is beyond me!'

'Don't let them hear you say so, then,' Claire commented. She finally let Brie go, promising she would creep into the room they were sharing, when the dancing was over.

Brie went upstairs and fetched a shawl

to put round her shoulders. The night was cool, but she was so hot in the hotel, she needed to get some clean air in her lungs. Bournemouth's bracing sea air was just what she needed.

The hotel was situated near to the cliffs, and there was a fine long promenade stretching high above the sea. That night the moon was full, a lover's moon, Brie thought, large and yellow and romantic. It cast golden fingers of light across the softly rolling waves far below the cliffs where she walked. The tang of the sea was heady, almost sensual.

Brie paused to lean on the railings, breathing in the scents of the night, unfamiliar to someone more used to city smells, and doubly welcome because of the fact. Two people passed her by, wrapped up in each other, not noticing her, the lovers this night enveloped...

'Beautiful, isn't it?' a male voice said beside her, and she felt her heart leap, not needing to turn her head to know whose voice it was. Her heart refused to settle down, continuing to beat erratically as Adam Andrikos leaned on the railings too. They must make a very intimate little picture, Brie couldn't help thinking.

'Are you intent on giving me a heart attack by creeping up on me like this all the time? That's the second time you've startled me,' she said crossly, whether he was her employer or not. If she'd been the nervous kind, her words might have been true. Adam laughed easily, a rich, warm sound in the night.

'If you were prone to heart attacks, I shouldn't think you'd have come to a sci-fi convention, darling.' He used the endearment as easily as theatrical people did. It didn't endear Brie to him. She had always thought it false, and took away its special meaning. Not that this man could call her darling in any other way but theatrically!

'What are you doing out here, anyway?' she said baldly. 'I'd have thought half the women in that hotel were panting to be your dancing partner—'

'Why do you think I was looking for you?' he retorted. 'We should get to know each other, since you're going to chaperone my sister—'

'You didn't trouble about checking me out before now. You left it all to your super-woman, Miss Lacey.'

Adam laughed softly. 'She is a bit

formidable, isn't she?' he agreed, as if determined to stay amicable. Where was this volatile Greek temperament that was so legendary, Brie thought suspiciously? Even between Adam and his sister, there had been reports in the tabloids...Brie thought her remark about his PR person was enough to send his temperature soaring, but he stayed calm...she was suddenly aware that his arm had slid around her shoulders, and she felt herself stiffen at once. She hadn't given him one little bit of encouragement. If anything, it was completely the reverse, and why pick on her, when it was as she said, and half the women at this convention were dotty over him? If not for the charisma of the man himself, then for the chance to be in one of his spectacular sci-fi TV productions, Brie thought cynically...

She gave a sudden gasp as the man twisted her towards him in one powerful movement. She had no time to think. Hardly able to breathe, she was in the hard circle of his arms and unable to break away. His hands rested on her slim shoulders for a moment, and then moved downwards, bending her towards him. Towards the possessiveness of his mouth, kissing hers in a sensual, passionate kiss...

For what seemed an eternity, Brie was held captive, both by Adam's embrace and the churning emotions inside her. Rage, shock, and an undeniable shivering excitement at the sheer magnetism of the man all vied with one another in her senses. She seemed to be held in time and space, as well as a very primitive basic need, overwhelmed by the night and the man and her own feelings.

Vaguely, out of the night, she was aware of footsteps passing by on the moonlit promenade. To those others, she and Adam would merely be two more lovers, silhouetted as one...she wrenched away from him, sliding her hands upwards between them to push against his chest. It was immovable, hard as rock, yet she could feel the heartbeats there, pulsing strongly, but never as rapidly as her own. She glared up at his face, shadowed now, her eyes blazing.

'How dare you do that! You've got a hell of a nerve!' She was no prude, but she was her own woman, and she chose who she wanted to kiss her. She'd had plenty of practice in keeping those amorous chinless wonders away from her on those huntin', shootin' and fishin' weekends at Lady Finola's.

Perfectly aware that Adam Andrikos, worldly as he was, might very well think her a naive little idiot, Brie didn't give a damn. Let him tell her the job was all off, and that he'd get somebody else to escort his young sister home to Corfu! If one of the recommendations for the job was to fall into Adam's arms, then he could forget it. It might have been briefly enjoyable, exciting even, but he was only buying her services, not her.

To her amazement, he let her go just as quickly, giving a laugh that was neither mocking nor angry. In fact, if it hadn't been so ludicrous, she might almost have thought there was a slight shake in it, as though he were as affected by that kiss as she had momentarily been. That really was crazy, Brie thought, when he must have had his fill of plenty of beautiful women!

'Ten out of ten, my angel of the evening,' Adam said in a calm, controlled voice. Brie stared at him, some of her own anger dissolving as her curiosity was caught.

'And just what is that supposed to mean?' she demanded suspiciously.

Adam leaned against the railings, no longer touching her.

'I know you think me a cold, heartless kind of brother, passing on my sister's care to a stranger, and not even interviewing you myself. Fact is, I have implicit faith in Miss Lacey, who's been with me for years. Added to which, my time has been so hellishly tied up lately, I could see no other way of hiring Susan's baby-sitter—' He caught the gleam in her eyes and grinned. 'Sorry. I should have said her chaperone, shouldn't I? That may be the dignified name for it, but it amounts to the same thing—'

'Adam!' Brie said warningly, hardly realising that she was using his first name. They seemed to have crossed the barriers of etiquette in one great stride, and there was no turning back.

His gaze ran over her, taut and tense still. The shawl had slipped from her shoulders, the flimsy blue dress clinging to her more revealingly than before in the fresh breeze from the sea. She shivered in the coolness of the air, and from his look, and couldn't have said which was the more emotive. She retrieved the shawl around her, tilting her chin as she did so in an unconscious gesture of defiance.

'Your photo didn't do you justice,' Adam went on in a slow, deliberately sexy voice. 'You looked young and fresh, and very pretty, of course, and your statistics told me you were perfectly capable of doing the job, and that was that as far as I was concerned. Miss Lacey gave you full marks.'

'So did you a minute ago,' Brie reminded him. She knew his kind of plausible line, she thought, and yet there was some devil inside her that made her want him to say more. His flattery meant nothing, yet she wanted it. This whole weekend was made up of crazy people, Brie reminded herself, and here she was, as crazy as any of them if she was going to let a little moonlight affect her...

When it came, his reply was nothing like she had expected, and she told herself it served her right for fishing for compliments.

'You looked too soft and warm and beautiful to be as efficient as you appeared on your application for the job. Once I saw you in the flesh—all that delectable flesh, darling—' she automatically stepped back a pace as he moved nearer to her, and he laughed softly again. 'I just had to prove to myself what kind of woman you really were, Brie Roberts. Whether your motives in taking this job were all they seemed, or if you thought it a neat little stepping-stone to get yourself a TV series—'

Brie couldn't believe this. The conceit of the man was impossible. She spluttered with outrage.

'You—you know what you can do with your job if that's what you think of me! You egotistical, chauvinistic—'

He grabbed hold of her arm as though he thought she was going to lash out at him. Brie wished she'd done so. She felt like hitting the handsome, self-confident face and letting him know that there was one woman at least who didn't think him Mr Wonderful...he snapped at her, the laughter gone.

'All right, I asked for that, but it wouldn't be the first time. Women can be pretty devious, and I've been taken in before by a pretty face—'

'Really?' she said sarcastically. 'I wouldn't have thought anyone could put one over on the great Adam Andrikos!'

Her heart was hammering now, so fast she thought she would probably keel over if it hadn't been that his hands were still gripping her arms. Still giving the impression of two people who were very close, Brie thought fleetingly, which just went to show how wrong such impressions could be.

'Anyway, you still haven't said why I scored ten out of ten,' she snapped back at him. He let her go.

'I need someone I can trust to take Susan home. She's not the easiest of children. She's aggressive and contrary, and I had to have someone young enough to whom she could relate, but not someone flighty enough to fall into the arms of the first good-looking man who made a pass at her—'

The arrogance of it almost left Brie speechless. She took a deep breath and spoke as evenly as she could.

'I see. And you're the irresistible, good-looking man I was supposed to fall for, is that it?' Her voice was like ice. 'All that passion in the moonlight just now was just some kind of test! And if I'd been fool enough to respond to it, I'd have got my marching orders. And you say that women are devious!'

She bristled with fury, and something else too. She hadn't wanted his kiss. Hadn't asked for it, or given him the slightest hint of a come-on. But she was still woman enough to smart at the thought that it hadn't meant a thing to Adam. He'd just been testing her. He was even more of a louse than she'd thought at first. She spun on her heel, intending to go right back to the hotel without another word.

He caught up with her before she'd gone a few paces, grabbing her arm again.

'All right, so it was a sneaky way to go about it.' He sounded irritable now, obviously not liking to be seen through so easily, Brie thought witheringly. Most women were probably so besotted by him, dazzled by his wealth, charisma, and the fact that he was the dishiest man for miles in any company, that they wouldn't look beneath the surface the way she had. She carried on walking, head held high, and Adam walked with her, his stride twice the length of hers.

'Look, slow down a minute, will you?' He snapped the order. Brie ignored it. 'So maybe I've learned not to take people at face value any more. It happens in a cut-throat business like mine. But if it's any consolation to you, I'm giving you my full support. I'd trust you with my sister anywhere. So stop being so damn obstinate and come and have a drink with me at the hotel. Come to the dance with me.'

Brie looked at him coldly. 'No thank you, Mr Andrikos. It wouldn't be a wise move on my part, would it? I might be tempted to drink too much wine. I might forget myself and hold you too tightly when we were dancing, and my ten out of ten would zoom to zero. Would you let go of me, please? Right now, the farther away from you I can get, the better I shall like it.'

She brushed off his arm, uncaring that he was her employer. For two pins, she'd throw up the job herself, if she hadn't wanted it so much, appealing to her in a way she hadn't expected. The poor little rich girl sister, with everything but a close, loving family at hand, and all the beckoning sun of Corfu...

Adam's words followed her, as cold as her own.

'And good-night to you too, Miss Roberts. I'm already deducting a point because of your rashness in tracking me down at this convention. Don't tell me *that* wasn't planned!'

Brie whirled round again, but already Adam was striding away towards the promenade, presumably needing to cool off. He still believed she'd come here expressly to meet him, she raged, and then felt a furious guilt because it was partly true. At least, it had tipped the balance when Claire had begged her to come!

She went into the hotel, still in a fury. The dance was in full swing. She could hear its raucous music, the noise, the laughter, everyone having a good time but her. She felt her eyes smart at the sudden realisation of how alone she felt, and knew she was being ridiculous. Nobody needed to be alone at this kind of convention! She only had to go and join Claire and Bill and she'd be welcomed to their crowd, and dance the night away. But she had never felt less like dancing. Adam Andrikos had seen to that. He was an insufferable man, and she hated him.

# CHAPTER 3

Away from the noise and in the stillness of her room, Brie felt herself gradually unwind. It had been a mistake to come here...and yet, perhaps not. Meeting Adam Andrikos had been something of a revelation. She didn't want to admit that there was anything admirable about the man at all. His exploits with women were legion, according to the tabloid press...until now, Brie had always been sceptical about such garbage, but now she was ready to believe anything. And yet...there had been ring of honesty in his voice when he'd told her the reasons for that sudden stormy kiss...and her own innate honesty told her that she was more than a little piqued that the kiss had not been on her own account!

Brie turned restlessly in the single bed nearest the window that she had bagged for herself, being first to bed. The large window pane was softly blue in the light of evening, and she could see the moonlight on the water from here, just by turning her head. It wasn't fair that something should be so achingly beautiful, Brie thought, reminding her of things she wanted to forget. As the tension eased, the snippets of memory wouldn't go away, assuming an importance in her mind that she didn't want but couldn't ignore.

Supposing she had met Adam Andrikos in any other circumstances? If they had been two people who happened to meet at an hotel at the coast, and been instantly attracted to one another, with a rapport and an empathy that drew them to one another's side the way a moth was attracted to a flame. If this had been some other kind of weekend, idyllically relaxed, and those two the only like-minded people here...how would it all have ended? Brie felt a shiver run through her veins. With a man like Adam, sensual and aggressively, charmingly masculine when he set out to be, it would probably have had only one ending...

Brie felt a sudden shock replace the delicious, tingling shivers of moments ago. What in heaven's name was she doing, letting herself dream of the man in this way? Letting her imagination take over to the extent of fantasising about him.

Wondering how it would be to be sharing a hotel room with Adam, no longer alone, warmed and pampered and loved...

The bedroom door burst open, making her heart leap in her throat. Claire snapped the light on, obviously completely forgetting her promise to be quiet. Brie glared at her, but it seemed that nothing could dim the sparkle in Claire's eyes tonight.

'Guess what's been happening downstairs? You missed a wonderful evening, Brie! I can't think why you didn't come to the dance. Your Adam Andrikos was there later, and he came over to Bill and me. It seems he's interested in making a series out of one of Bill's books. Isn't it fantastic? Bill's on top of the world—' She paused for breath, seeing that her friend was less than enthusiastic. 'Hey, I'm sorry if I woke you up. Though how anybody can sleep on a night like this beats me. Didn't you want to soak up every second of tonight?'

Brie looked at those shining eyes behind the glasses, and didn't have the heart to dampen that glow by being scratchy. She struggled up in bed. She wasn't going to get any more sleep yet anyway, with

Claire as excited as she was. She'd barely drifted off, and she still wasn't sure if her dreaming had been of the wide awake variety or in her subconscious. Uneasily, she didn't want to know. Maybe Claire's chatter would get him out of her mind.

'It's all right. I was only dozing. I had a bit of a headache, which was why I got some air and came on to bed,' she said quickly. 'Tell me all about it then.'

Claire didn't need a second invitation. While she undressed, she chattered. While she plugged in the kettle and made them both some coffee, she chattered. By the time Brie was almost dropping with sleep and Adam's virtues were being extolled to the nth degree by the admiring Claire, she knew she was happy for her friend, who had apparently found her soul-mate in this Bill Jones/Diablo Hades, who was now going to be involved in a TV series with Adam Andrikos, and was on cloud nine at the thought. There had to be many discussions in London about the new script and locations, so Bill would be down there frequently in the next few weeks, and wasn't it wonderful? Claire didn't have to wait for her transfer to the York library branch to be seeing him again.

'It's wonderful, Claire. I'm very happy for you,' Brie mumbled. 'Now do you think I could close my eyes for an hour or so before the whole thing starts up again in the morning? Unless I decided to stay in bed all day—'

'You can't do that,' Claire squeaked. 'Adam's taking his seminar, and you've got to be there for that. It begins at ten in the morning.'

Brie groaned. 'Then shut up, will you, and let me get some sleep,' she moaned. She'd only taken in half of Claire's excited news, but it was all wonderful. Everything was wonderful. She was still muttering how wonderful it was for Claire's benefit when she slept at last.

Morning came all too soon. The room seemed to be crowded with people. Garish costumes and smiling faces and loud-talking men in elegant dark clothes, with flashing white teeth and self-confidence oozing out of every pore, filled the room. Brie gasped, disorientated for a few seconds, until she realised it was the TV set in the bedroom, and that Claire was turning up the sound so that she didn't miss a minute of it.

'Oh good, you're awake,' Claire said unnecessarily. 'I've made some tea. I knew you wouldn't want to miss this. We're on breakfast television, Brie. Last night's do—oh, there's Bill—'

Clearly, she wasn't seeing anyone else. Brie sat up in bed and took the cup of tea Claire handed her. She may as well give in, though where Claire got all this unexpected energy was beyond her. She was normally such a little mouse...Brie gave a sudden gasp as Adam's handsome, teak-brown face filled the screen, smiling out at her in a way that seemed intensely intimate, as if he was seeing no-one but her. Instinctively, Brie pulled the sheet up beneath her chin without realising it.

Adam's eyes looked out at her, the camera catching every fleck of colour in them. They were dark, velvet brown, but with little highlights of gold where the bright lights reflected in them. Laughter lines fanned out from the corners when he smiled for the camera's benefit. His presence was undeniable, his voice a rich smooth experience as he answered the banal questions with an expertise Brie could only admire, remembering the frenetic urgency to get someone on camera, to track down the successful, the rich, the famous...

Brie gasped again, feeling her cheeks flood with colour as Claire squealed out her name.

'Brie, it's you! How gorgeous you look. That dress was exactly right for you—'

Brie felt a stab of alarm. The girl in the blue dress smiling in embarrassment as she sat beside the suave darkly handsome TV producer looked to her exactly what she was, naive, compared with him; hating every moment of being pushed into the limelight; and too much the adoring little slave, Brie thought in sudden anger. How could the camera have captured such a moment when she was looking so archly at Adam? Had she ever looked at him that way? It could only have been for a fleeting moment, but the TV cameras had managed to record it...

'Oh no,' she groaned. 'He'll love this!'

She wasn't sure if she meant the words seriously or not. She was sure Adam was the kind of man to preen himself on any woman's adoration. In her case, it wasn't what he wanted. He expected her to be a prim little schoolmarm, suitable chaperone to his wayward sister...and it wasn't a true assessment of Brie's character at all! Not that she was any *femme fatale*, but she didn't fancy his other labels either. She felt the quick anger begin to burn in her all over again, for tagging her in that way. His 'angel of the evening', who was obviously meant to be Miss Purity as well.

Was that the way he really saw her? Brie felt a strange resentment inside her. Was she so sexless, so unattractive to him that he could kiss her the way he had, and feel nothing? While she, who hadn't wanted or welcomed his kiss, had felt sensations curling inside her that were new and exciting, that had been as disturbing as if she had been transported to some fantasy world like those conjured up by the sci-fi writers themselves. She had been lifted high out of reality, to some other plane, to a world consisting of moonlight and fragrance and the rushing of waves on the shore...she caught herself up short, aghast at the way her thoughts were spinning. All this for *one* kiss? And how dare he have dismissed it so casually, when it had had such an impact on her...?

Brie ran her tongue around her suddenly dry lips. Until that moment, watching the TV screen and seeing the camera quickly pan back to Adam again as being of more importance than a mere pretty honey-blonde by his side, she hadn't acknowledged that the kiss had had *that* much impact. But now she found herself watching that mobile mouth, as though she could taste every sensual line of it, knowing its shape, its texture, its warmth on hers...

'—my angel of the evening, you mean,' Adam was saying, bringing her senses back to reality. He was speaking about her to the interviewer. Claire's chatter made her miss half of it then in her excitement. '—yes, she'll be escorting my sister to our home on Corfu.'

'It was all right then,' Claire was saying. 'He didn't mind that you were here after the funny interview you had with his PR person?'

'What?' Brie had to drag her thoughts to Claire. Had Adam tucked her hand in his arm after that last little statement? Had the TV camera spotted it, homing in on it so that a few million breakfast TV viewers could see it too and put their own interpretation on their relationship? She couldn't think straight. All she could think was that the interview on TV had sounded ultra-cosy. As if Adam was making no bones about her being his current girl-friend. It sounded as if the home on Corfu was *their* home, hers and his. How could he be so stupid?

But that was just it. He wasn't stupid at all. Brie doubted that he ever gave an interview that was so careless...unless the carelessness was intentional. She was getting so muddled...but she had a fast-growing suspicion that if Adam let the viewing public think that Brie Roberts was the new girl in his life, then it was done quite deliberately. And thinking more astutely now, she wondered if it was all those millions he was getting at, or one viewer in particular. She tried to think. Wasn't there some talk about Adam and some lady script-writer a while ago? Was all this charade for her benefit? She wished she could be more positive about it, but she rarely kept up to date with the goings-on of media people. She left all that to Claire.

She opened her mouth to ask her friend, and then closed it again. She didn't want to know. If there was any dirt in Adam's life, then it was his business and Brie had no intention of making it hers. Her only involvement with him was to do a job. She was escorting his sister Susan to Corfu. She knew it was no more than that, and so did Adam. And if any TV people came sniffing around her for more juicy information, they'd be sadly disappointed, Brie thought savagely.

'I'm getting up.' She threw the bedcovers off and went into their bathroom to shower, leaving Claire glued to the screen as the sci-fi people paraded for the cameras in their weird costumes. Claire was clearly enchanted by it all. Brie was rapidly wishing she had stayed at home. She had no desire to get caught up in any kind of political double-dealings Adam Andrikos may have dreamed up. He'd have been surprised and suspicious at seeing her here, and she allowed that. But turning it to his advantage by hinting at some liaison between them was something else. And something that was quickly going to be squashed if Brie had anything to do with it.

She dressed in a cool shirt and white jeans, sliding her feet into stack-heeled mules to give her a little height, but which were still comfortable. Today would be spent listening to lectures and discussions, anyway, so there was little walking to be done. In the following morning there would be only informal coffee get-togethers, an A.G.M for the business side of the sci-fi fraternity, and home after lunch. Brie hoped she'd get through that much with Adam around. Or maybe after his own talk, he'd be going home, she thought hopefully. And wondered just where all that so-called dreaming empathy of last night's fantasising had vanished to!

She brushed her hair to a gleaming fall around her shoulders, and pinned it at each side with a tortoiseshell comb. Light make-up to finish, and she was ready, feeling businesslike, cool and ready to tackle anything. And 'anything' meant Adam Andrikos! Claire rushed around, having spent too much time with the TV, and was flushed and flustered by comparison, but already twittering at the thought of seeing her Bill again.

How would they all appear this morning? Brie wondered as they went down in the lift to the hotel dining-room. More garish outfits to torture the eye...? She felt a real shock as they walked in and found two empty places for breakfast. Where were all the painted, horrendous, spectacular beings of last night? The Terror Lagoon people, the gold-paint and sequins, the green slime effects...here was a buzz of noise from industrious, serious-faced people, some decidedly middle-aged to elderly. Impossible to believe that they were the same...but true!

'There's Bill!' Claire waved frantically, and the nice-faced young man of last night turned out to be quite ordinary too. Except in Claire's eyes. Clearly, they both looked at each other through rose-coloured glasses, Brie thought, feeling her throat constrict. She'd never seen love at first sight in action, but she knew she was seeing it now, and it couldn't happen to two nicer people...

'Sorry you couldn't make it to the dance last night, Brie,' Bill was saying. 'We missed you.'

I'll bet you did, Brie thought, hiding a grin. She tried not to look around the room for Adam. She didn't care whether he appeared for breakfast or not...

'You won't see Adam this morning,' Bill seemed to be reading her thoughts. 'Speakers get the royal treatment for the meal before their seminars. He'll be breakfasting in Room X.'

Before Brie could say airily that she really hadn't noticed that he wasn't here, someone else stopped at their table. She just managed to associate the small grey-haired lady with the Witch of the Winds of last night, and her name-tag pronounced her Author of Seven Sci-Fi Novels and One Film-Script. Brie began to feel quite humble by comparison.

'Have you seen the morning papers? We've got a good spread. They're all on sale at reception, Di.'

Di? Brie realised she was referring to Bill/Diablo as Di. The quirk at the corners of her mouth threatened to broaden, and she hid it with her napkin. They were all so serious! But she supposed there could be no other way to make their preposterous stories sound real. Sci-fi was big business, and not to be taken lightly, or written with tongue-in-cheek, she told herself severely!

'I think I'll skip breakfast,' she said quickly, knowing she had to get out of there fast. 'I'll go and get the papers and see you both in the sun-lounge, O.K?'

She got no objection from Claire or Bill, as expected. She doubted if they even saw her leave. She went to reception and bought three papers, so they could swap round later. The sci-fi convention was covered in varying degrees of importance, but all had plenty of photos as Brie might have predicted. The costumes were a photographer's dream—or nightmare in some cases. There were snippets of author interviews, hopes and aspirations. There was sci-fi jargon spilled about in appalling puns by bright young journalists who would undoubtedly make some of the authors cringe and make the old hands say cynically that any publicity was better than none. There was Adam Andrikos, smiling out at her...

Brie had turned the page in one of the papers, and there was Adam. And there beside him, a petite fair-haired girl with large eyes and soft mouth, smiling happily as though she'd just scooped the biggest story of the century herself. And underneath was the caption, 'Adam Andrikos and his lovely Angel of the Evening at Sci-fi convention. Is Adam star-struck at last? From the way he's holding on to his lovely lady, we would say so. She's soon to go to his beautiful Corfu home. Watch this space, as the sci-fi fanatics would say...'

Brie felt as if all her nerves were constricting at that moment. If they tightened up much more, she'd shrivel up and disappear altogether. And right now that wouldn't be such a bad idea, she thought wildly. All the people who read this rag would be getting totally the wrong idea about her. And Adam had fed them with it, the furious thought ran through her mind. At least, he hadn't stopped it. He hadn't made it plain enough why she was going to Corfu, or if he had, then his actions and the ridiculous way he'd squeezed her hand and looked into her eyes had simply belied the simple truth as far as the newshounds were concerned. They had scented a story, and she was in the middle of it!

Brie crunched up the newspaper in her hand. It made no difference, of course. There were scores of others being handed round. There were thousands all over the country, all linking her romantically with Adam Andrikos. Adam's new girl...she closed her eyes so tightly that they hurt. When she opened them again, the sun-lounge was starting to fill up with the breakfasters, prior to taking their seats for the morning lecture. The elite from Room X, the organisers, the committee, the morning speakers, all were gracing the peasants with their presence...

She was becoming more cynical by the second, Brie thought in amazement. It wasn't her usual style at all. Adam had provoked it. She saw him before he saw her. Just for a change. And she could no more stop her heart from beginning an erratic little drum-beat than stop the sun following the rain. She watched him enter the room. He had a predatory walk. She hadn't noticed that before. He wore black, tight-fitting trousers this morning, very expensive-looking, and a black and white striped shirt tucked into them and all bonded together by a very macho black belt with a huge gilt buckle that must have weighed several pounds...he was the flamboyant one this morning, Brie thought, yet it was in such an understated way. He oozed self-confidence and sex appeal. He could be a very dangerous man for a woman to get entangled with. She would be the one to get hurt...to be left picking up the pieces...she sensed that he would be as ruthless in love as in business. It showed in the tigerish way he paused and looked all around the room, knowing his target and having no time for anything or anyone else...

Her heart jolted again as his eyes stopped roving as soon as they met hers. She should have known she was his target, though why he was making such a play for her she couldn't imagine. He must have plenty of people here all dying to fawn over him, while Brie couldn't be rid of his attentions fast enough. Not altogether true, the treacherous little voice inside her said. At least, if he had been anyone else, it might have been different. As it was, she despised his methods, his family callousness, his total charisma that was making half the people in the room follow his progress towards her.

Most of them would have seen the morning papers, Brie thought in a flash. Adam reached her as the thought swept into her mind. He leaned down and kissed her lightly on the mouth, his hands pressing into her shoulders just enough to stop her twisting away from him. Anyway, the kiss was so brief that it was over before it had begun. She wondered if he even guessed how branded she felt by his merest touch...

'What do you think you're playing at?' she glared as he sat down on the settee beside her and slid an arm along the back of it as though they were very intimate indeed. This whole convention probably thought they were here on an illicit weekend by now, Brie thought in mortification. She glared at him as he smiled into her eyes.

'Haven't you seen the papers? I can see that you have,' he nodded towards the small pile of them at her side. 'We should give them their moneysworth, don't you think?'

'No, I don't,' Brie snapped. 'And after your remarks last night, I don't understand what's going on. I got ten out of ten, remember, for being the prudish little chaperone. What role are you casting me in now, Mr Great God TV Producer?'

Adam grinned. 'All right, I deserved that. I suppose I'm trying to make amends for my clumsiness—'

'By letting half the country think I'm your new live-in girl-friend? Thanks very much. I think I'll take the prude tag—'

'I hope you won't. There's too much

fiery woman in you to be such a martyr, Brie, and that's an objective statement. Take it as a friendly observation. Some lucky man is going to love that wild spirit of yours. You have the cool looks of an angel, but underneath you're all warmth and fire, and that's what every man is looking for in his woman.'

Brie's heart was thudding against her ribs as he spoke, so fast it made her feel sick for a moment. He spoke so objectively, just as he said, and yet for a burning, timeless moment she wanted him to say it was the way *he* felt about her. Not some lucky, faceless man in the future who would appreciate her womanliness, but *him*, Adam Andrikos, sitting there smiling at her so complacently that she could lash out and hit him.

She had felt like that once before. What was it about him that stirred up these turbulent emotions? She wasn't normally filled with such aggression, such a need, a compulsion, to hear him say in that arrogant way of his that she was *his* woman. She must be going mad. He seemed to bring out all that was worst in her. All the primitive, wanton feelings she didn't even know she possessed. Not like this, anyway. Other men had wanted her, desired her, loved her, but she had felt none of this strange, confused mixture of feelings towards them. One minute feeling the strongest affinity between them. The next, positive that they were poles apart, and could never meet sensibly on any terms.

'Are you coming into the lecture?' Adam was saying prosaically. Brie became aware of a ringing in her ears. Bells were ringing now? Wasn't that the way the romantic novels described it...? She realised it was the bell for the morning lectures to begin, and that Adam was holding out his hand to pull her to her feet.

Feeling utterly foolish now, she put her hand in his without thinking, and was pulled close to him for an instant.

'I have to rush back to London right after my lecture, Brie. Unfortunately, I can't stay for the whole weekend after all, much as I'd like to. I've no doubt we'll be meeting again soon. Say hello to Susan for me.'

She was confused again. He still held her hand. Someone appeared in her line of vision, a camera popping, as one of the sci-fi people asked to take their photo and did so without waiting for an answer. Brie was past caring who took her photo now. Adam was leaving that morning. She should be glad, but as she got swallowed up in the crowd moving towards the lecture-room and lost sight of Adam as he was ushered towards the platform, she felt the oddest pang inside. She was disturbed by his presence, but without him, all the scintillating sci-fi nonsense in the world would dim. He was that kind of man.

She saw Claire waving, and slipped into a seat beside her and Bill. Next minute, the convention chairman began introducing their very special and distinguished guest speaker, the noted TV producer of top-rating sci-fi series, Mr Adam Andrikos. Brie felt a ridiculous rush of pride as Adam got to his feet amid roars of applause, and seemed to smile directly at her for a moment.

The noise died away, and from then on, Adam became the top-rating speaker of the convention. He spoke with such authority on the way their two media complemented each other, the words provided by the authors, the visuals by the TV technicians, that everyone there warmed to him and respected his expertise. Brie could only admire the way he dignified the whole proceedings. What may seem laughable to the sceptics, the dressing-up, the strange language of the sci-fi novels, the earnest discussions of characters and plots that were out of this world in every sense...Adam made sense of it all, and was adored by all.

His voice was a pleasure to listen to, melodic and rich. No-one nodded off when he talked. No-one took their eyes from that handsome face except when he used his hands to illustrate a point. He had beautiful hands, Brie thought. Not beautiful in any feminine way, but beautiful all the same, strong and capable and expressive. They had held her close. She could still feel the warmth when he had pulled her to her feet, the tingle at the contact...

Hers were the only eyes to waver from the speaker's face at that instant. Suddenly she couldn't look at him, for fear he would catch her eye and see the sudden flush in her cheeks, the tell-tale realisation that something she hadn't bargained for was happening to her.

She wouldn't let it happen, Brie thought, in a kind of panic. She didn't believe in love at first sight. Love should grow slowly, like a plant nurtured by the sun and the seasons to make it strong and healthy before it blossomed to maturity. Love at first sight wasn't to be trusted...except in the case of Claire and Bill, she was forced to admit, who were already behaving as though they were on some other planet. The one thing Brie had never imagined was that it would happen to her.

She was appalled that the thought should even enter her head. Love between herself and Adam Andrikos just wasn't possible. That there was an undeniable physical attraction was something else. She couldn't close her eyes to that fact, nor deny that he could rouse her to passion or anger faster than anyone she had ever known. But that wasn't love. She needed to know someone properly before she could love him...and besides, the down-to-earth side of her nature protested, it would be the greatest folly to let him ever think she could fall for him.

She could just guess his reaction to that. Her rating would plunge immediately. Her ten out of ten would be wiped out, she'd lose the job on Corfu and worse than any of that, Adam would no doubt see her as someone with ambitions to get into TV by the back door...or by way of the producer's couch. Did that still happen? Brie wondered. Whether it did or not, she wasn't giving Adam the chance to accuse her of it. Her job was due to last a month, and then he'd be going to Corfu himself and she would be released.

She had likened it to a jail sentence before. It would be even more so if she was condemned to be near him every day, so she had just better be quite sure she was well away from the island on the day he was due there.

Brie heard a great roar of applause and realised that Adam's talk was over, the questions done, and she'd missed the last part of it altogether. She had been too taken up with her own anxieties, not the least of which was that her angel's halo was in some danger of slipping when the little devil inside her asked her who she thought she was fooling? Love at first sight was an accepted fact of life, but for once she wouldn't look life in the face.

## CHAPTER 4

Looking back on it later, Brie had to admit that the rest of that weekend fell pretty flat for her. Not for Claire, of course, who was somewhere up on Bill/Diablo's cloud with him. But Brie was quite glad to get back to London, and to start thinking about packing for the month in Corfu. This time, with more mixed feelings than before. Then, it had merely been a job, an exciting one, with all the perks of foreign travel and sun, and the certainty that she was well able to cope with any thirteen-year-old, however capricious!

Now, everything had changed. There had been no communication from Adam although she had half expected it. There was just the formal letter from the PR person, with the tickets for the flight and details of the arrival on the island, when Brie and Susan would be met by a member of the Andrikos household. Miss Lacey herself would be at the airport with Susan Andrikos to hand her over. The officious wording made the girl sound like some unwanted parcel, Brie thought sympathetically. And she sensed that Miss Lacey hardly considered all this part of her own PR duties, but complied because Adam Andrikos asked her to. He had undoubtedly charmed her into it, Brie thought, and admitted that it would be hard to resist...

She closed her suitcase with a bang, having to sit on it to fit everything in. A month was still a month, even if most of the clothes she was taking were light-weight cottons. The villa was bordering the beach with a small village nearby within walking distance. There would be plenty of time for sunbathing and shopping, since she didn't imagine she had to wetnurse Susan every minute of the day. Just what she *was* supposed to do with her, she wasn't quite sure, except that Miss Lacey had said a proportion of each day had to be spent in study, since the child had done so badly in her recent school exams. Miss Lacey was a very pompous lady, Brie had decided there and then, and she didn't imagine there was much love lost between her and Susan.

She grew more nervous as the day of

departure approached. Even a little put out because Adam had sent no word himself. Why should he? the sane part of her asked. She was just an employee with whom he'd had an amusing interlude. If Brie was foolish enough to read any more into it than that, she was heading for trouble. All the same, the memory of the kiss was still burned deep into her memory, and she told herself repeatedly how glad she was that he'd had to cut the weekend short after all. If not...yes, she was definitely glad, Brie thought fervently.

She and Claire hugged each other effusively when Brie's taxi finally came, courtesy of Adam's office, regardless of the distance to Luton airport. Claire would miss her...but since Bill was coming to London for four days the very next week, Brie didn't think she'd spend too much time moping. And she couldn't be happier for Claire. She positively shone these days. Bill had phoned every day, and the two of them were obviously head over heels in love already. Brie felt a small pang of envy. How wonderful to love someone like that and be so loved in return...how wonderful...

'Be sure and write to me and tell me everything about Adam's villa,' Claire squeaked as she usually did when she was excited. 'You never know—if Bill gets to do his own screenplay for the TV series, we might even get out there ourselves one day. Corfu sounds beautiful!'

'I'll write and tell you everything,' Brie promised. The taxi hooted, and she grabbed her suitcase and holdall, suddenly wanting to get out of there before she got cold feet about the whole thing.

Suddenly she had the most extraordinary feeling that she was burning her boats, which was absurd. It was a month's work, that was all! A month in the sun...

The traffic was heavy, the taxi driver talkative. Brie wished he'd keep his eyes on the road instead of constantly glancing over his shoulder to talk about the weather, the price of food, the national balance of payments...she felt ready to wilt when they reached the airport, and it wasn't a good feeling, knowing she needed to keep her wits about her to meet Susan Andrikos.

She was only a child, for heaven's sake, she reminded herself. But a child with quite a formidable reputation, by all accounts, even according to Adam, who was supposed to be fondly attached to his half-sister. She signed the chit for the taxi driver, to be sent to Adam's account, and looked around. She spotted Miss Lacey at once, thin and efficient, her hair as severe as the clothes she wore. Some PR lady...but maybe she was super at promoting her boss's interests, if not herself.

Brie was more interested in the girl standing sullenly beside her. Susan Andrikos. She was as dark as Adam, and beautiful in an immature, sultry way. The Greek heritage, of course. Though she was not that immature, Brie saw at once. There was an air of defiant self-confidence about her, from the flashing dark eyes so reminiscent of Adam's, to the full red mouth that was surely not solely as nature intended...to the well-filled school uniform that the girl probably hated. Miss Lacey had collected her from her expensive boarding-school, so she would only have her term-time changes of clothes in the small leather grip by her feet. Brie walked forward, annoyed to find she was taking a deep breath as she did so.

Miss Lacey's face changed miraculously to an expression of relief as Brie approached.

'Good-morning, Miss Roberts,' she said

crisply. 'I was beginning to get anxious. The traffic was heavy, I suppose. This is Susan, as you'll have gathered,' she went on without wasting time on niceties. 'They'll be calling your flight in about fifteen minutes, so unless there are any last-minute queries, I'll hand her over to you and wish you both *bon voyage'*.

Just like that. Brie saw the girl's face glowering at being dismissed so quickly. Miss Lacey might be a wow in business matters, but she hadn't the faintest idea how to deal with adolescents, Brie realised.

'I don't have any, thanks to your efficiency, Miss Lacey,' she said at once. 'Unless you do, Susan?' She looked directly at the girl, drawing her into the conversation. For a second she thought she was going to get no response at all, then there was a defensive mutter.

'Yes. Why can't I go home by myself? I'm not a baby. Why does Adam treat me like one?' She glared belligerently at Miss Lacey and then at Brie.

'Now you know your brother wouldn't let you go all that way by yourself, Susan—' Miss Lacey began irritably, not hiding the fact that she was anxious to get away from there.

'I promise not to treat you like a baby, Susan,' Brie said coolly. 'In fact, since there's no porter about, how about finding me a luggage trolley and we'll dump all our stuff on it and then check in? We've left it pretty late.'

Susan's eyes clashed with hers for a moment and then she shrugged. There were plenty of trolleys nearby, and she moved away to fetch one. Miss Lacey's face was disapproving.

'Watch her, Miss Roberts,' she advised. 'She's just as likely to run off if you give her too much leeway. It wouldn't be the first time.'

'Maybe it's time someone started trusting her then,' Brie said. She didn't like Miss Lacey. And despite Susan's obvious aggression, she fancied she glimpsed something far more than mere obstinacy behind the girl's petulant pout. Brie had had enough experience with children to wonder if there was some deep unhappiness there too. She was no psychologist, but some psychology was part of her course, and besides that, she felt instinctively that Susan Andrikos was the victim of too much money and too little love.

There was no time to ponder on such

matters now. She should have checked in her luggage a long while back, and was forced to take the last two seats available, wedged in between other people. Susan had wanted a window seat and couldn't have one, and it wasn't a very good beginning. They walked out to the plane together a little later on, and Brie could feel the antagonism from the girl as though it were tangible. She decided that straight talking from the beginning was the best way to handle the situation.

'Look, Susan, I'm sorry if I was thrust on you like this, but I assure you I'd have liked to get to know you sooner, only there was no time. I gather the last lady who—er—accompanied you to Corfu couldn't make it this time—'

'*Wouldn't* make it, you mean. She couldn't stand the sight of me.'

Brie stared at her. She spoke matter-of-factly, uncaringly, yet Brie still had the feeling that she cared very much. Only the brittle shell she'd built around herself wouldn't let her admit it.

'I can't believe that—'

'You'd better believe it then. You'll end up feeling the same way. Everybody does.' She looked directly at Brie then.

She had a disconcerting habit of looking at a person unblinkingly, as if she could see right through them. It was the same way that Adam did it, Brie remembered, with a little jolt inside.

'Are you Adam's latest?' Susan said, loud enough for the people around them to hear and glance their way as they climbed the steps into the plane. Brie felt the colour tinge her cheeks. It was obvious that the girl was trying to shock her by her rudeness. She was enough to put anybody off, but Brie was darned if she was going to put *her* off.

'Would it bother you if I was?' she said, with an amused little laugh that hid the way she fumed inside. It was Susan now whose face went a dark red. She gave an exaggerated shrug as they found their seats, and clamped the seat-belt around her, folding her arms tightly across her stomach, her hands clenched into tight fists.

'Why should I care? Adam can do what he likes. He doesn't care about me, so why should I care about him?' Her eyes swivelled round to Brie for a quick glance. 'You're not his usual type. He usually goes in for actresses and script writers and people like that, not ordinary girls.'

Even a precocious thirteen-year-old with too much money should have learned better manners than that, Brie thought angrily.

'I'm really not surprised people don't care about you, Susan. You don't give them much of a chance, do you? And you seem pretty ordinary yourself, and rather boring too. If you can't think of anything more interesting to talk about than your brother's affairs, I'd prefer it if we didn't talk at all.'

She could see Susan's mouth dropping open at this, and guessed that the girl's lack of manners normally produced anger or shock or even tears. It wasn't going to happen with Brie. She turned to the lady sitting next to her and began talking about the flight and Corfu, and ignored her charge altogether for the next ten minutes. Until she realised how tensely Susan was sitting in her seat as the engines began to roar and the plane began its race down the runway prior to taking off. The quick glance at Susan's sickly face told her that the girl was scared stiff, and too defensive to show it. On an impulse, Brie grabbed her hand.

'I hate this bit, don't you?' she lied. 'Once we're up there it's marvellous, but this taking off bit is horrible. You won't tell anybody I was scared, will you?'

Susan shook her head, not speaking, but she didn't snatch her hand away either. As soon as they were airborne, Brie let go of it naturally, and didn't miss Susan's audible sigh of relief when the need to keep seat-belts fastened was over. It wasn't much of a victory, but Brie felt they had established a tiny bond all the same.

'I haven't been to Corfu before,' she told Susan conversationally. 'You'll have to show me around. All the best beaches for swimming and so on—'

'We have our own private beach,' Susan said, as though she were saying they had an apple tree in the garden. It obviously meant nothing to her. 'I'm supposed to be doing lessons every day, anyway—'

'Not all the time. There'll be plenty of time to do other things,' Brie said, as the scowl returned to Susan's face.

Over lunch, Susan began to perk up. The flight was well under way by then, and her nerves were obviously settling down. She looked at Brie from beneath her rather heavy, well-shaped brows. When she frowned, they drew together in an almost straight line.

'Why did Adam choose you, anyway?' she said pointedly.

'He didn't. Miss Lacey interviewed me,' Brie told her evenly.

The girl gave a short laugh. 'Oh, Miss Toffee-nose may have interviewed you, but Adam chose you, didn't he? Adam always chooses my baby-sitters,' she said bitterly. 'And anyway, you can't fool me on that one. I watch TV all the time. I have one in my room at school, even though the headmistress doesn't like it. I saw you and Adam on breakfast TV last week, so don't fool me that you and he aren't—you know—'

Brie felt a hot wave of colour race up her cheeks now. The little madam was goading her as far as she dared. That stupid sci-fi convention! She wished she'd never gone to it. No, she didn't. If she hadn't gone, she wouldn't have met Adam Andrikos, and the thought was in her head before she could stop it. *He* had been in her head ever since last weekend. She couldn't get him out, however much she tried. She had even dreamed of him twice, and she didn't want to think about that either!

Sensible, feet-on-the-ground Brie Roberts wasn't used to coping with what amounted to almost erotic dreams about a man she hardly knew!

'I didn't meet your brother until last weekend, Susan. You should know enough about media people to know how they love to romance about people. I'm sure your brother's told you enough about them in the past—'

'What about the newspapers then?' Susan didn't hide the triumph in her voice. 'Some of the girls smuggle them into school, and we all saw you with Adam in that stupid picture. Angel of the Evening, or something, they called you. Sounds as crackpot as those other weirdos dressed up as little green men—'

Anger swept through Brie so fast she could have shaken the girl until her teeth rattled. As it was, the blaze in her blue eyes as she turned on Susan was enough to stop the girl in her tracks.

'Why don't you shut up and let me enjoy the flight, you irritating little girl? And those weirdos dressed up as little green men, as you call them, indirectly provide all the luxuries you have, let me remind you. They provide the words for the series

Adam produces, so just remember that next time you feel like sneering at them!'

Susan's lips clamped together. Any good she'd done by pretending to hate take-off was probably undone, but Brie didn't care. She knew exactly why none of Susan's chaperones had lasted long if this was a sample of her manners.

'All right,' it came out viciously. 'I just wish I didn't have to sit here with you, that's all. Why couldn't Adam have flown me home in his own plane? He can always find time to fly any of his girl-friends about, but not *me!*'

Brie was acutely embarrassed at the way the people around them were looking their way, a few of them whispering. Maybe they'd seen the TV or the newspapers, and had realised who Brie was. She felt her nerves jangle. The month ahead stretched interminably. Even sun and sand and the blissful island of Corfu couldn't compensate for four weeks in Susan Andrikos' company. Did she have to be quite so resentful of Adam? It didn't make sense to Brie, unless there was some deep-seated childhood reason of which she was unaware.

As far as Brie was concerned, it

wasn't a comfortable flight because of Susan's constant irritating remarks. Brie was thankful when the descent began. Then, regardless of her companion, the thrill of excitement ran through Brie again. Below was the verdant island of Corfu, an emerald in a sapphire sea, fringed with golden sand. The reputed Garden of the Ionian Sea...the island certainly appeared fabulously green and fertile, in contrast to what might be expected of dry, dusty Greek islands. Claire had read up on it at the library, typically Claire, and had told Brie she must try some of Corfu's oranges, reputedly the best anywhere, and the wild strawberries...

The plane touched down smoothly, and there was the sound of seat-belts unfastening. Presumably Susan was unperturbed by landing, and she peered through the window of the plane, as if she expected their driver to appear immediately.

'Who will be meeting us?' Brie asked.

Susan spoke carelessly. 'Probably Miguel, or maybe Stavros. They both work at the villa. Miguel's wife, Juanita, looks after the place, except when there are large parties there, when they get extra help from the village.'

'Is that often?' Brie asked. It seemed like another world to her, yet Susan seemed to take it all for granted. The rich probably had no comprehension of what a working girl's life was like, she thought wryly. Clearly, this girl would never need to worry about money. It was ludicrous to feel slightly sorry for her, yet that was the feeling uppermost in Brie's mind right then. Susan had everything far too easy, which was probably why she appreciated none of it.

'Depends how often Adam's around,' Susan stated. 'If he's in the mood to have business meetings here, it can be quite interesting. Sometimes he manages it while I'm home for the holidays, so I get to meet some of the TV people. But it's all pretty boring really when they just go into huddles about scripts and casting and lighting problems.'

Susan was evidently trying to sound blasé, and merely succeeded in sounding petulant. Brie guessed that Adam did his best, but had no real idea how to cope with a fast-growing teenager, rebellious and lonely. In Brie's opinion, Susan was definitely lonely. She had seen that mixture of temper and frustration, that mistrusting, bewildered look, enough times in other children not to know it. She had been trained to see it.

They walked off the plane, and the summer heat was intense, with just enough of a balmy breeze to prevent it being stiffling. After the cool of an early English summer, Brie found it like a little bit of heaven. What a place to come to for a job! Her spirits rose, despite the antagonism emanating from Susan Andrikos. She wouldn't need to be with the little madam twenty-four hours a day, Brie consoled herself, and there would be times when she could get away and relax blissfully in these idyllic surroundings. No wonder Claire envied her...

She wanted to drink in everything at once, the brilliant green of the vegetation, the dazzling blue of the sky, the scent of a foreign land that was always so tantalising to British eyes and ears. The British abroad, Brie thought, smiling at her own exhilaration. Like kids let out of school...

She caught Susan's eye. Not this kid, though. This one didn't look as though she had a scrap of excitement in her body. There must be something, someone, about whom she was enthusiastic. Apart from Adam, when he deigned to be around, of course...

They got through the customs formalities, and Susan led the way out of the airport, far more competent than many of the adults hanging about uncertainly. Brie followed, pushing their luggage on a trolley until they reached the outside.

'There's Miguel,' Susan said at once. 'He and his wife are Spanish, but don't let that fool you. They're more Greek in their habits than half the natives on Corfu!'

The middle-age man in casual shirt and jeans came across from a modest-sized car, not a limousine as Brie had half expected from Susan's lordly ways. Miguel smiled broadly at them both, showing masses of white teeth against a tanned skin. He reeled off a welcome that was a strange mixture of Spanish and Greek, that Susan seemed to follow instantly, before his smattering of English. The girl responded at once.

Brie stared in disbelief as she seemed to come to life as though someone had switched on a thousand light bulbs inside her head. She was suddenly animated, a child again, instead of the pseudo-adult she attempted to be. She raced ahead of them.

Brie walked to the car, and immediately saw the reason for Susan's burst of excitement. There was a large shaggy dog jumping over her in the back seat, its tail beating furiously with excitement. Susan's arms were around his neck, hugging him while his large pink tongue licked her with delight. Obviously, this was Susan's Achilles' heel...

Brie got in the front seat at Miguel's suggestion. There was no room in the rear anyway.

'Isn't he gorgeous?' Susan shouted above the beating of the dog's tail, and his exuberant barking. 'Adam gave him to me when he was just a pup, and if that stupid school would allow pets, I'd take him to England with me and never have to be apart from him!'

'He'd have to go into quarantine for the first six months,' Brie said practically, and Susan glared at her.

'I know that, but I'd wait that long if I could have Pottsy with me at the end of it, but I can't. I'd change schools to find one that allows pets, but Adam won't let me—'

Brie could hear the bitterness creeping into her voice again.

'You'd better make the most of him for the next few weeks, then. I'm sure your brother knows what's best for you regarding schools—'

'Why do grown-ups always have to say that?' Susan scowled, her arms still around the dog's neck, but her eyes flashing angrily now. '*I* know what's best for me, and it's not that stupid school! Why can't I go to a school here? And why do you keep calling Adam "your brother" instead of using his name? I'm sure you got friendly enough to call him Adam at that weekend you spent together!'

She was insolent, suggestive, and Brie felt the hot colour run over her face at the sideways glance Miguel gave her. She was furious at needing to defend herself, and she did so in a quietly controlled voice.

'That weekend was a convention, Susan, and I was not there with Adam. I hadn't even met him before. And you should be worldly enough by now to know that newspaper people often put their own interpretation on a situation. We happened to be sitting next to each other at dinner, and it gave the photographers an interesting bit of gossip, that's all—'

'I saw the breakfast TV programme too,' Susan put in rudely. 'I heard Adam call you his angel of the evening, and it didn't sound as if the two of you had just met to me!'

'Well, since I don't have to answer to a rude little thirteen-year-old for my actions, you can just think what you like,' Brie said pleasantly. 'And if you can't think of anything to say that's less hostile, then I suggest you say nothing at all and let me enjoy the ride.'

She turned her back on her and caught the edge of a smile of Miguel's lips. Still, Brie wondered uneasily how discreet he was, and how much of what Susan had been reckless enough to say would be bandied about among the staff before very long. She gave a mental shrug, hoping that they knew enough of Susan's tantrums to ignore much of what she said.

She looked around her, ignoring Susan completely, who appeared to have gone into a fit of sulks now. Miguel pointed out the bays along which they drove smoothly, the fine white villas dotted on the hillsides, the jewel-like flowers in abundance everywhere, lush and brilliantly scarlet, magenta, sapphire hues. Dark green spears of cypresses mingled with the rustling silver-leaved olives and the rich hedges of flowering aloes dividing many of the properties more naturally than fences or walls. They drove to the south of the island, and the scents of pines and herbs, orange and lemon groves seemed to drug the senses. Wonderfully aromatic in air that was as clear as wine, Brie felt that she would never tire of breathing deeply, expanding her lungs to enjoy all the benefits of the island. She was going to be so healthy by the time she left Corfu, she thought jubilantly.

'There's the villa,' Susan spoke up from the back seat, apparently recovered from her outburst with the help of Pottsy, still slobbering all over her.

Brie looked, and just managed to refrain from gasping out loud. It was beautiful, magnificent in its stark white simplicity, with terraced gardens leading right down to the private beach. Superlatives raced through her head as Miguel drove towards it. And the one certain thought was that if she owned a place like this, she would never want to leave it. She had an instant sympathy with Susan, even if the girl's dislike of her English school had little to do with her love of home. Brie could learn to love a villa like this very easily...

'Impressive, isn't it?' Susan was still trying to sound blasé. Or maybe she wasn't merely trying. She must have seen this scene a thousand times, the sudden rounding of the corner to where the white villa dominated the skyline, the sheer beauty of the setting with the terraced gardens and the startling contrast of golden beach and indigo sea below. The sheer luxury of it all...

'Someone is waiting for you,' Miguel's deep voice said as he pulled the car to a halt in the circular driveway. Susan groaned.

'Not the tutor already. Adam could have given me a few days to get over this rotten term—'

Her voice stopped, and as Brie turned to open the car door on her side, the brilliance of the afternoon was momentarily blotted out by a large masculine body reaching for the door handle on the outside of the car. Brie's heart jolted as though a million volts had shot through it. The car door opened, and she stepped out into the sunlight.

'What are you doing here?' She heard

herself stammering as inanely as any schoolgirl. As gauche as Susan Andrikos should be...

She heard another car door being wrenched open, and before she got an answer, Susan had rushed past her like a small dark tornado, followed by the wildly excited Pottsy. And just for a crazy moment, Brie too, had the absurd desire to throw herself into the wide-spread arms that were enveloping both child and dog...

Above their heads, Adam Andrikos smiled down at Brie, a slightly mocking smile that said he was the kind of man who would turn up anywhere, any time. Expense and distance meant nothing to his type of man. Realising it widened the gulf between them in Brie's mind, despite the way his look was taking in every bit of her appearance in the thin, warm-weather clothes, and noting the sudden heat in her cheeks at the unexpected sight of him. It was no more than a natural reaction, she told herself, when she had fully believed him to be in London, and to be there for the next four weeks. Wasn't that the sole reason she had been hired?

'Welcome to my island, angel,' Adam

said softly, and Susan twisted her head to glare savagely at Brie as the words vibrated against her as she clung tightly to Adam a minute more. With one sentence, Adam had undone all the careful confidence-building Brie had been attempting ever since they left London. Now, Susan very definitely believed Brie to be 'Adam's latest'...

# CHAPTER 5

'I'm sorry if I startled you,' Adam said lazily, his arm still loosely around Susan's shoulders as the three of them walked towards the cool maarbled terrace of the villa. 'Fact was, it suddenly became necessary for me to bring some of the technicians over here for a few days, and what better time than now? There was no time to let anyone know—'

'So I could have come with you in your plane, instead of—' Susan began rudely, shushed up by her brother with a reproving look.

'You see why my sister has need of a calming influence, Brie? She leaps off the handle at the slightest provocation, without ever thinking things through.' He looked severely at Susan. 'No, my sweet, you couldn't have flown home with me, because we had a full load. Besides, I didn't hire Brie just for the ride.'

Brie looked at him suspiciously. He was too bland, too smooth, too everything. And it was too much of a coincidence that business should bring him here like this. He hadn't expected to be here for another month, and then she had presumed it to be a holiday visit to round out Susan's school vacation. She was as precipitate as Susan at that moment, not thinking things through...

'Anyway, now you're here, I don't have to do lessons every day, do I?' Susan pleaded, ignoring Brie altogether. 'And I don't need a nursemaid either!'

He gave her a playful smack on her rear. 'That's a matter of opinion, sweetheart. And yes, you do need to have lessons every day. Miss Vesey will be here tomorrow—'

'She's at least a hundred years old!' Susan grumbled.

'Then you should be very thankful to have someone young and pretty around the place,' Adam retorted, a remark that didn't seem to endear him to his sister from the darting glance the girl shot at Brie.

How many other 'young and pretty' girls had been brought here, ostensibly for Susan's benefit, and in reality for Adam's? Brie thought suddenly. Well, if he had any funny ideas about Brie being the next notch on his belt, he could think again. She wasn't falling into that trap.

She was already wary of him now. He'd made it plain that he suspected everyone under the age of forty of wanting to get into TV by the back door, and clearly thought Brie capable of it too. It was crazy to think that her own looks and personality were working against her in that respect. She could just imagine what would happen if she once succumbed to his charms. He'd be waiting for her to demand a contract. Crazy was the word for Adam Andrikos...yet Brie could still feel a certain sympathy.

Just as Susan was the poor little rich girl, with everything she wanted except people with enough time for her, maybe Adam too was the victim of his own success. Maybe he had been let down badly by someone he loved very much. Even as she thought it and caught the quizzical look in his eyes at that second as she looked around the villa in admiration, Brie asked herself if she was the one to be going soft in the head. Adam didn't need anyone's sympathy.

'Does it meet with your approval, Miss Roberts?' Again, that slight mocking note in his voice, sending the flush to Brie's cheeks. She decided the direct approach was best, and looked at him candidly.

'You must know perfectly well that I'm impressed. You obviously live very well here and don't go short on anything. But please don't treat me like a child, Adam. I'm not dazzled at the thought of working for a TV producer. I've worked in the homes of titled people, and no matter how much money they had, or what their status, I soon discovered that under the skin they're still people, the same as me. And some are a darn sight nicer than others,' she added coolly.

He grinned down at her. His face became infinitely more attractive when he smiled, less stern and more animated, the Greek in his personality accentuated by the dancing lights in his dark eyes and the gleam of his teeth against the tanned skin.

'Oh, I can be very nice, angel,' he said, softly enough so that only she could hear, his fingers running briefly up and down her bare arm. Brie jerked away at once.

Susan had been prowling about the room, re-orientating herself with familiar surroundings, and glanced at them suspiciously as Brie's face showed her annoyance.

'Do you two always fight like this?'

Susan asked, her voice a little high in her attempt to sound worldly and slightly bored. 'I thought lovers were supposed to be loving towards each other!'

Brie drew in her breath with anger. She really was the limit. A darn good hiding was what she needed! Before she could snap out as much, Adam had answered, seemingly unconcerned, but with a crispness in his voice that Brie guessed Susan knew well enough to heed.

'So they are. But since Brie and I don't come into that category, you can rid yourself of any little romantic notions about us, Susan. Go and tell Juanita we're here, will you? Ask her to bring some tea into my study for me and my people there. You and Brie can have some later. I daresay Brie will want to get unpacked first. She's in the blue room overlooking the beach. I thought she'd appreciate the view. Think you can manage to show her there?' He was faintly sarcastic, as if daring Susan to be any more insolent.

In answer, she clicked her fingers at the large shaggy dog, sitting patiently on the floor all this time, and spoke carelessly.

'Sure. As long as Pottsy can come with us. I'll go and tell Juanita.' The dog jumped up adoringly, ready to follow.

When she had left the cool airy room, with its mosaic floors and scatter rugs and deep-cushioned chairs, Adam looked at Brie.

'I'm sorry about her,' he said, more naturally than usual. 'I know you were thrown in at the deep end, and she does have appalling manners at times—'

'It's all right. Really it is. I've dealt with some very maladjusted kids in my time—' Brie spoke quickly, wanting to reassure him for some reason, and rid him of the sudden worried frown that had appeared between his brows. Wanting the smile to come back...he was vulnerable where Susan was concerned, she discovered to her surprise. And in wanting to reassure him, she'd as good as implied that Susan was one of those unfortunate maladjusteds...

'I'm sorry,' she floundered. 'I didn't mean to say that I thought Susan was that bad—'

'She probably is,' Adam said drily. 'We've all had blinkers on for far too long where she's concerned, but now that she's reaching adolescence, the situation's changing. I didn't believe she could be so temperamental, blowing hot and cold the way she does, one minute loving and gentle, the next, like a little tornado!'

Brie hadn't seen much of the loving and gentle yet, except where Pottsy was concerned. But she felt a rush of warmth at the preplexed look in Adam's eyes, and the sudden way he ran his fingers through his thick hair. Tycoon he might be, but there were still some things where a woman's sensitivities scored over a man.

'It's part of the female character, I'm afraid,' she said sympathetically. 'The most frustrating time of a girl's life, I suppose. The only comfort I can give you is that we all grow out of it, and the only advice I can give is to try to be as patient as you can, and—and be around when she needs you.'

She didn't know if she should be talking to him like this. He was her employer, and from the way Brie herself had reacted to him on the occasions they had met so far, she couldn't blame him if he thought her as temperamental as his own half-sister! But that was different. And listening to her own words, she realised she was as good as asking him to stay...and from her own viewpoint, she wasn't at all sure that that was a good thing.

She didn't hate him any more. She realised it almost to her own surprise. She had been perfectly prepared to hate him, having been interviewed by his super-efficient Miss Lacey and sent on what Brie half thought of as an errand of mercy. Now, having met the man, and met the girl, her feelings had done a very swift changeabout, and it had happened without her even being aware of it.

Neither did she want Adam to have any inkling of the fact that if he was vulnerable where this sister was concerned, then so was Brie vulnerable where he was concerned. And it just wouldn't do! Hadn't he said that he'd suspected her of wanting this job for her own reasons? Giving her that ridiculous test to see her reactions...and giving her ten out of ten for refusing to be swept off her feet by him...

How would he feel, knowing that ever since they had met at the sci-fi convention she had been unable to get him out of her mind? How would he react if he was aware that she had had what amounted to erotic dreams about him, and that kiss in the moonlight on Bournemouth's cliffs had been merely a sweet prelude to such fantasies that made Brie hot all over to think about them...?

'I'll do my best,' Adam was saying gravely, as if taking her advice was important to him. 'I do try to be at home when Susan's on vacation, but you realise it's not always possible. My work has a habit of getting in the way of the things I'd prefer to do.'

She began to feel embarrassed at speaking to him so freely, but at least they were communicating on some other level than the merely sexual. Powerful though that was, it could sometimes be more of a nuisance than an asset, blotting out friendship, affection, sympathy. Women needed all of those things in a relationship, Brie thought, while for a man...she stopped herself thinking that way. Their only relationship was a working one, and their only interest was in Susan's welfare, and she had better remember that. Why would Adam Andrikos, TV tycoon, wealthy, dynamic, with any woman he wanted, ever want a relationship with Brie Roberts? Unless it was for an amusing interlude... and that was not the kind of love Brie wanted. Hers was the once-in-a-lifetime variety, and when she met her soulmate, it must be the same for him too...

Susan came back to the room with Pottsy barking noisily, breaking the mood, to Brie's relief. The atmosphere had become altogether too intimate between the two of them, moving subtly from a business arrangement to a mutual discussion of Susan's welfare. Like proxy parents, in fact! It was one thing to be glad they were communicating, but the thought of their becoming too much involved on Project Susan was an uneasy one. Presumably Adam would be here for a very short time, and then she'd be left to pick up the pieces. And knowing only too well how unpredictable a teenage girl could be, Brie didn't relish the thought.

'O.K. Tea's ordered,' Susan said breezily. 'I'm going up to my room to change out of these hideous clothes. I'll show you yours, Brie.'

She didn't wait for a reply, and Brie followed her up the long curving wrought-iron staircase to the next floor. Susan threw open a door, and Brie immediately knew why it was called the blue room, from the lovely pastel carpet and curtains, the white walls and pale-coloured wood furniture. Through the long windows that opened out on to a small balcony, there was a fabulous view of the beach below the gardens. In the bay, several white-sailed yachts seemed to be motionless on the brilliant blue sea, while farther out a luxury liner cruised steadily south. The entire panorama spelled out the good life, and Brie took a sudden deep breath, exhilarated. She was here, and she was going to enjoy it.

'Juanita said she'll bring you some tea up here in a minute,' Susan said. 'You can have it on your balcony if you like.'

'I don't want to put her to that trouble. I can come down—'

Susan shrugged. 'She's bringing it up. My room's in the other wing. If you want me, you only have to buzz me on the intercom, but I don't see that we need to meet again before dinner, do we? I am allowed some time to myself, aren't I?' The resentment oozed out once more.

'Look, Susan, let's get it straight once and for all. I'm here for a month, so we may as well get along, or we're both going to be miserable. You can do whatever you want within reason, but Adam's paying me to be a—a companion to you, I suppose.

So why don't we try to be friends instead of enemies?'

'Why should you want to be my friend?' Susan said rudely.

'Because I think you're in need of one. It must feel a little strange to you, coming back home, and leaving all your friends at school. I daresay you're out of touch with people of your own age around here—'

'I don't have any friends at school, and I don't have any here,' she said flatly.

'Don't be silly. Everyone has friends—'

'I don't. People don't like me. Don't you know that by now?' The shimmer of tears was gone from her lashes so fast as she blinked furiously that Brie wondered if she'd imagined it. 'And you're not my proper friend. You're paid to be nice to me!'

She turned and ran out of the room. Brie stared at the door after her. Now she knew she was right. Susan was a very mixed-up adolescent, and had probably been hurt by people, or just by life itself. She couldn't resent the girl's rudeness at that moment. She felt desperately sorry for her instead.

The tap on her door a few minutes later brought Juanita with her tea and a plate of iced biscuits. The Spanish girl was large and plump and a good bit younger than Miguel, and seemed to be permanently smiling. It was good to see someone so normal!

'Thank you, Juanita. I'm in need of that.'

'It's my pleasure, Miss,' she said in her quaint pretty accent. 'Dinner will be at seven-thirty tonight. Mr Adam and his gentlemen ask that you join them for a glass of sherry in the lounge at seven o'clock. Is there anything else for you?'

Brie smiled at her. 'No thank you. Except—can you tell me how I get down to the beach from here?'

'Is easy, Miss. You walk around to the side of the villa and there's a nice walk between the trees to get you right to the beach. It takes you five, six minutes only, even if you go as slow as the snail.'

'Thank you,' Brie laughed. 'I think I'll take a walk there before dinner then.'

Even before she took a shower and changed into more formal wear, she thought. She was glad she'd had the foresight to bring some cocktail dresses, though she hadn't expected to need them so soon. She hadn't expected to see Adam here...the little warm glow she couldn't help ran through her at the thought. And immediately she decided not to wear the same dress she'd worn at the convention. She wanted no reminders of that night, especially since her photo had been splashed around the newspapers, and she had been seen on breakfast TV looking into Adam's eyes, wearing that dress...the memory of it could still get her nerves jumping. Being thrust into the limelight like that was something that must take a bit of getting used to, Brie thought.

She unpacked quickly, drank her tea and sampled the iced biscuits. If they were home-made—and they appeared to be—then Juanita's cooking was definitely to be recommended. She left her cup on the tray and went out of the room, finding her way downstairs easily. There was no sign of Susan, but since the girl obviously wanted—and needed—some time to herself, Brie wasn't too concerned. She too needed time to get used to her new surroundings.

The walk to the beach was a shady, tree-lined meander. It was no time before Brie suddenly emerged into the dazzling sun-trap of the beach, the sands glinting, the waves curling softly onto them with a gentle kissing sound. It was sheer bliss, it was private and secluded from any roads, exclusive to the villa Andrikos. One could swim naked at midnight here, with only the moon and stars to witness it. The thought was at once erotic and immensely attractive to her. The beach was gentle shelving, perfectly safe, and on an impulse, Brie slid out out her sandals, and walked along the water's edge, letting that silken water lap her toes and feeling the delicious tingles pervade every pore.

She glanced up at the villa, beautiful in the sunlight. What a wonderful place to live, with the terraced gardens a riot of flowers in every colour imaginable, the balconies all around with their windows thrown open, inviting the sun inside and not keeping it out, like so many shuttered houses on the continent did. Brie warmed to the ambience of the place, unconsciously identifying it with its owner. Yes, he was warm too, warm and vibrant and alive. He complemented his home. When he wasn't there, it would seem emptier, less colourful, more lonely...

She gave a shaky little laugh, knowing there were only the sea-birds to hear it. How fanciful she was becoming, and how sweetly and insidiously Adam Andrikos was becoming part of her life, whether she wanted it or not. And how dangerous it was to let herself dream of him in any other way but as her employer. She wasn't falling in love with him...she wasn't fool enough for that...but the physical attraction between them was very powerful, and she wasn't fool enough to deny that either. The physical, and something more, which was very important to Brie.

Adam, of course, would only be experiencing the physical, and she reminded herself that she had better believe it. Brie glanced back at the villa, understanding just why Susan resented having to leave it to go to boarding-school in England, where it was so often cold and rainy, instead of being here where it seemed to Brie that the sun must constantly shine. Common sense told her it couldn't always be like that...

She drew in her breath at a sudden movement on one of the balconies of the villa. A man had been standing motionless, watching her. Tall, broad-shouldered, dark-haired...even from here, Brie knew at once that it was Adam, and she felt as gauche and vulnerable as if she really had been bathing naked in the moonlight. It was absurd to feel that way, but it was the effect he seemed to have on her. She was oddly perceptive of him, and she didn't want to be. She didn't want to be at all.

She turned away from the water's edge and made her way back across the warm sand, only stopping when she was in the lee of the tree-shaded lane leading to the beach to brush the sand from her feet and slide them into her sandals again. Her footprints trailed away from her. They looked lonely. One set of footprints in the wet sand always did...Brie gave an irritated sigh. Her thoughts were doing credit to Claire lately. Claire would say she'd been reading too many library romances, the way she herself did in between the stints of sci-fi books. Claire would say knowingly that Brie must be falling in love...

'I certainly am not!' She said the words aloud. 'I don't know him well enough for that, and what I know about him is enough to put off any sane woman!'

Her subconscious answered her crisply. Claire didn't know Bill/Diablo either, but any fool could see the stars shining in Claire's eyes whenever she spoke of him. And when did love make distinctions about the suitability of the recipient, anyway? Brie struggled with her subconscious. He was too high-powered a man for her tastes. He neglected his sister. He was too casual about hiring someone to be her companion, and the frequent changes in Susan's life were in danger of turning her into a total neurotic at thirteen. Brie blamed Adam for that. He was also too smooth with women. His reputation with them had gone before him, whether the tabloid newspapers had exaggerated or not. He was bad news. She gave him zero out of ten, and smiled at her own assessment.

She was still smiling, thinking that she had discovered the best way to keep Adam Andrikos in his place, by listing all his faults, when she turned a bend in the lane and came face to face with him.

'I thought it must be you,' he said at once. 'I was fascinated by the way the sunlight lit your hair, and the delicate colour of your skin. You must be careful, Brie. Don't underestimate the power of the sun here. I'd hate you to get burnt.'

'Thanks for the warning,' she hadn't expected to see him, and his words caught her off-balance. She wasn't sure if there was a double meaning in them or not—and his compliments had the oddest way of coming out rather flat at times, his voice abrupt. It was almost as though he was saying it against his will—and why should the smoothie A.A trouble about that?

'You must try a swim at midnight,' he went on, and Brie started, wondering if he could have read her thoughts earlier on. 'It's quite safe, and no-one comes here except the people at the villa. You've brought a swim-suit, I hope?'

This time she didn't miss the way his gaze darkened as he let it roam over her shape, not missing a single part of her until she felt that he would be able to trace her contours blindfold. She resisted the urge to wrap her arms around her body to escape that bold look, but she felt the needle-sharp tingle of annoyance, and admitted that there was a feeling of something more too. She was human, for heaven's sake, and what woman wouldn't respond to the fact that a man was telling her plainly with his eyes and every bit of body language at his disposal that he desired her?

'Yes, I've brought a swim-suit,' she said jerkily. 'I'll probably do as you say when there's no-one else around—'

Adam laughed, lounging against the bark of a tree, insolently male.

'Oh, I thought we'd make up a beach party and have a barbecue down there tomorrow night, Brie. Never let it be said that you thought I was co-ercing you into being there alone with me!'

Now he was making her feel stupid, and she'd asked for it too. She had been in control of her own life for a long time now, and in control of other peoples' children too. So why the feeling of inadequacy whenever Adam was around? It wasn't the way she liked to feel, and she laughed too, more naturally than she felt.

'I wasn't meaning that!' she said, hoping he didn't guess that that was exactly what she had meant. 'I just didn't want to step out of line, that's all. It's not *my* beach—'

He reached out and squeezed her arm. It was only a light touch, and was just meant to be friendly, Brie guessed. There was no earthly reason why it should send tremors running through her. It was as though his slightest touch could ignite a flame inside her. The knowledge of it shook her.

'It is your beach, any time you want it,' Adam said quietly, and this time the nuances in his voice were saying much more than the words. They were telling her it wasn't only his beach he was offering...any time she wanted it...Brie felt her mouth go dry. The memory of his ridiculous test kept drumming in her head. It was her head she should be listening to, not her heart, because that was telling her something very different, leaping in response to the dark look in Adam's eyes...she moved imperceptibly away from him, as though the small distance was going to make any difference to her confused emotions. She muttered a brief thank you and made to pass him. His arm shot out and closed around her waist, effectively stopping her. If she moved on, she would only be more imprisoned by him.

'Don't fight me, Brie. You're a very beautiful girl. We can be friends as well as employer and employee, can't we?' She heard the faint teasing note in his voice and guessed that he knew exactly what he was doing to her. It would be part of his stock-in-trade, she thought. The beautiful island and the beautiful girl...how many of them had there been before her? she wondered. And how many of them had managed to resist?

'I've no objection to being your friend,' she said, with as much dignity as she could muster. 'But that's as far as it goes. Isn't that what you wanted of me? A capable person to be Susan's companion? I'm sure you wouldn't want me to forget the conditions you put on me in Bournemouth. I certainly haven't forgotten—'

'Ten out of ten again, angel,' Adam said dryly, but he released her at once. Everywhere he touched her, her bare sun-kissed arm, the small span of her waist...Brie felt as though her flesh throbbed with new life, as though his touch had the power to electrify her.

'Can I go now, please?' she spoke distantly. 'I want to shower and change for dinner. My feet are full of sand.'

'Of course. Don't let me keep you. I'll see you later.'

He strode on down the lane towards the beach, and Brie went back to the villa. He had the power to unnerve her too, she admitted. She could never be immune to the man, and they were destined to clash if he really tried to make a pass at her. He had made it all too clear that if she responded it would be the end of the job, and Susan would have yet another temporary companion. Yet she was willing to stake her life on the fact that he'd go on trying. It was going to be a battle of nerves, and the only consolation was that he surely wasn't going to be around here much longer. Brie didn't really know why he had come now. With some of the TV people, apparently, the technicians...she still didn't know why he'd picked this particular day, but she didn't like it one bit.

She wandered out on to her balcony for a few minutes, where the early evening scents of flowers were out of this world. She breathed them in deeply, letting their fragrance wash over her. Away in the distance, against the silver-blue glitter of the sea, a lone figure seemed to be following in her footprints. Adam. Brie watched him as he had watched her, and had the curious, inexplicable feeling at that moment that he looked a lonely figure. Solitary and alone...she dismissed the idea at once. He probably needed time to be alone. All creative people did. There was no reason on earth to think of Adam Andrikos as lonely, but reason didn't always play a large part in her thinking lately...

# CHAPTER 6

The talk at dinner was apparently an extension of the meetings that had been going on in London and ever since Adam and the TV technicians had arrived on the island. There were three of them, two portly men smoking fat cigars who looked at Brie through screwed-up eyes every now and then, and a younger man, thin and intense and hanging on every word Adam said. If Brie had thought this was going to be an ordinary kind of dinner, she was discovering that where business was concerned, Adam's thoughts strayed nowhere else, and she grudgingly gave him credit for that.

Not that he hadn't complimented her on her appearance when she came downstairs for sherry in the lounge, and was introduced to the men. Susan was already there, wearing a shiny top and matching pants that were much too old for her. Her eyes dared Brie to make any comment. Brie wore a simple white silk dress with several gold chains at the neckline, and high-heeled white sandals. The men were dressed semi-formally, and as usual Adam's presence overshadowed them all. Dark and handsome in black figure-hugging trousers and roll-neck white silk shirt, he would grace any society dining-room, Brie thought fleetingly. No woman could look at him without feeling a certain pleasure, merely because of his virile attraction. He caught her glance, and she looked away in flushed embarrassment.

'Adam won't let me have sherry,' Susan had complained loudly. 'It wouldn't do me any harm, would it, Brie? You ask him, and then I can have some.'

She was a clever little minx, Brie thought. Trying to get Brie on her side. Trying to force some conflict between them. And intimating all too clearly to the TV people that if Brie asked a favour of Adam, he'd surely grant it. It lumped them together very neatly.

'It's up to Adam, Susan,' Brie said coolly. 'It's not part of my job to suggest you start drinking at your age—and besides, I've always made it a policy in my other jobs never to come between the children and their families.'

She heard Adam give a chuckle as Susan's eyes flashed angrily. It put her strictly in her place, and established Brie firmly as the childrens' nanny...not an image she had ever felt went necessarily with tweeds and a school-marm appearance, but right now it suited her very well to remind everyone at the villa that she was here to do a job and nothing else. In particular that she wasn't here for Adam's entertainment.

Juanita announced dinner while Susan was still visibly sulking, and trying to get the intense young man to tell her something about outside location work. He was clearly not used to precocious girls of Susan's age, and trying in vain to brush her off without being obviously rude about it. He looked very relieved when he was placed at the opposite end of the table from Susan, and next to Brie. She wondered if it was deliberate that Adam was directly opposite her, so that she could hardly avoid looking at him between mouthfuls of the delicious sea-food Juanita served up.

'We'll take a drive to the north of the island tomorrow then,' Adam told his guests. 'I think you'll find the terrain ideal for the background, Les. It's very mountainous with outcrops of limestone, and rugged to the point of being barren in places. It'll suit the script perfectly in my opinion, but you must all agree on it before we finally decide.'

Brie's interest was caught. The man Les, one of the portly technicians, shrugged his massive shoulders expressively.

'If you say it's O.K, I reckon there'll be no problem, Adam. You know the landscape better than we do, and we've always been able to rely on your judgement before. But we'll need to take a look, of course, and Stanley will want to see what the lighting angles are like—'

Stanley, the intense young man, nodded, as Susan turned excited eyes on her brother.

'Are you going to film something on Corfu?' She was bubbling, suddenly just an excited thirteen-year-old instead of the *femme fatale* she was trying to be.

'We may do,' Adam smiled. 'It's not definite yet, but the background of the book we're going to script for the new series seems to match perfectly with what we've got right here. We may do some prelims in the next week or so—'

'That means you'll be home while I'm here!' Susan went on, her eyes glowing. 'I could have come home on my own this time, Adam. I didn't need Brie to bring me!'

'You need her to teach you some manners,' he said calmly. 'And I certainly won't be here for the whole month. A few days now and then, maybe, so don't start making plans for picnics and things. If I'm here, it'll be to work, Susan.'

His eyes moved back to Brie's. She had been wondering the same as Susan. If Adam had known about this possibility of Corfu being used as the next filming location, why bother hiring her? But as he said, he wouldn't be here the whole time, and perhaps the idea had come up suddenly. She doubted too, whether he was in the habit of confiding in Susan about his work schedule. The thought that he was going to be here at all was more disruptive to Brie's equilibrium than she had expected. It hadn't been in her plans. A month to chaperone Susan Andrikos, if that was the right word for it, and then back to England, without ever any need to see or even meet the arrogant and objectionable Adam Andrikos, who could farm out his sister to a stranger without apparently a second thought.

But all of that had changed, before Brie had even arrived here. She had already met Adam at the sci-fi convention and got off on the wrong foot with him. He'd given her that stupid test, and made her afraid of admitting even to herself that she found him the most exciting, shiveringly, attractive man she had ever known, and that she was drawn to him like a moth to a flame. She had discovered that he had vetted her after all, which slightly modified her opinion of him as heartless. She had been pictured in newspapers as his angel of the evening, and seen herself on TV at the convention with him, looking for all the world as though they were very special to one another. And he had held her in his arms and kissed her...and if the earth hadn't exactly moved, it had certainly shifted a little...

Brie swallowed some of the chilled white wine in her crystal glass, feeling the cool liquid trickle down her throat and change to fire. It epitomised the way she felt when Adam gave her one of his burning looks. She could be cool as ice, but his sensual gaze was enough to fire her blood...

'How long do you propose being here this time, Adam?' Les went on. 'I have to be back for a meeting in London in a couple of days—'

'We'll go back the day after tomorrow,' Adam said. 'We'll take the day to go up in the mountains tomorrow, then I thought we'd have a beach barbecue tomorrow night to shut my little sister up,' he grinned down the table at her as he spoke, hearing her whoop of pleasure, 'then we'll fly back to London early next morning.'

'Do you think we can get the writer to come over next week?' David, the third man, asked.

'I hope so. He's been in London a week or so now, and seems pretty keen to work with us, though I think we're going to need a script-writer to tidy up some of his stuff. He's not used to TV work, and he may need careful handling—'

'He's not one of these prima donna writers, is he?' Les growled. 'The last one couldn't bear to have a sentence altered, it you remember—'

'Oh, I think Hades will be agreeable,' Adam said positively. 'He seems a nice enough bloke, and I heard somewhere that he was getting married soon, so his mind will probably be on other things besides his precious script. We can talk him round, even if he has to baby-sit every episode.'

Brie felt her nerve-ends jumping. Hades? There couldn't be another sci-fi writer with that surname, could there? And if it really was Diablo Hades, alias Bill Jones, then if he was thinking of getting married soon, poor Claire was about to have her heart broken into little pieces.

'Is that Diablo Hades you're talking about, Adam?' she asked quickly. 'I believe I heard someone say you were talking to him at the sci-fi convention.'

'That's the man. Do you know his books?' Adam asked in surprise. 'I'd have thought they were a bit gory for your taste.'

'Brie looks more like the romantic novel type,' Les grinned, intending it to be a compliment. Brie just managed to avoid glaring at him, hating to be type-cast because of her looks, and what would he know about her reading tastes, anyway? She didn't like him at all.

'I've never read his books, but I met him briefly at the convention,' she ignored Les and spoke directly to Adam, being deliberately vague about meeting the writer in the hope of learning more.

'He's a bit of a dark horse,' the other man, David, obliged her. 'Bland as they come when you meet him, but his books are filled with powerful scenes and promise to make good series material. You'll do well to sign him up, Adam.'

How much more of a dark horse was Diablo/Bill? Brie thought uneasily. Adam's words had shaken her. Had the writer been on the brink of marriage when he'd met Claire? If so, he'd kept it very quiet...as David said, a dark horse...

Her thoughts whirled. Dimly, she heard Susan's young-old voice pushing into the conversation far more than she should, and wondered vaguely if she should try and divert her. She wasn't sure that was her role. The girl was sometimes impossible...it was also hard for Brie to remember that she had been orphaned a little more than six months ago. Susan gave no hint of mourning, or of the fact that this was the first time she had been home since their parents' deaths. She was a very strange, self-contained and brittle girl. If someone ever got beneath the brittle shell, what then...?

Adam was reprimanding his sister himself, and Brie let her thoughts come back to matters of more personal importance for a moment. Diablo Hades, who had made no secret of his attraction to her friend Claire...and her friend Claire, going around with stars in her eyes and obviously feeling she had found her soul-mate. Claire wasn't a strong enough character to withstand the blow it would be, if Diablo/Bill had just been stringing her along at the convention. Brie felt positively sick at the thought. She cared a lot for Claire, and had always felt protective towards her. That feeling was uppermost now. Her child-care training coming to the fore, she thought keenly, and not wanting Claire to get hurt...

The TV talk washed over her. Susan was wrapped up in it all now, more animated than usual, and apparently because she expected to see more of Adam after all. Brie felt a burning resentment sweep through her. In her mind Diablo Hades, Adam Andrikos, the cigar-smoking men...they were all part of the same kind of men. Ruthless, out for their own profit, living for the moment and uncaring what hurt they did to other people. Her growing feelings towards Adam were vanishing fast, and if there was no real reason to put them all in the same category, Brie wasn't looking for reactions. She felt too upset at the thought of Claire's reaction when her Bill didn't want to see her any more.

Or maybe he would. Was that the way some of these people carried on? She thought of the unknown fiancée presumably tucked away somewhere, and spared her a moment's pity. But the bulk of it went to Claire, and Brie knew she would have to warn her, however painful it was going to be.

'Why can't Brie and I come with you tomorrow?' She realised there was some tension at the dinner-table now, while the upsetting thoughts had spun in her head, and that Susan and Adam were glaring at one another. The TV people were seemingly unconcerned, and Brie guessed that they were used to temperaments like these.

'You can't, and that's an end to it,' Adam snapped. 'We're here on business, and we'll be back in time for the beach barbecue. You and Brie can organise it with Juanita. Les and David won't want to be bothered with you being around. Besides, there's no room in the truck, and it won't be a comfortable ride. We need to see how the locations fit in with the Hades script, and *Planet of Darkness* calls for some pretty wild backgrounds—'

By now Brie had gleaned that Les was the Special Effects Director, and David was Senior Stunts Co-ordinator. Stanley, the younger man, was a whizz with outside camera work, despite his unlikely appearance. To Brie, he looked more like an insurance clerk...

'I think you're rotten, and you always leave me out?' Susan suddenly burst out, her eyes blazing. Adam's mouth was fast tightening into a furious line, and he reeled off a string of Greek sentences to his sister that no-one else could follow.

If it was meant to quell Susan, it didn't work. She rattled off an answering stream in Greek that had Adam getting to his feet and ordering her out of the room until she could behave herself.

'I haven't finished my strawberries,' she raged.

'Yes, you have.' Adam moved quickly round to her side of the table and picked up the dish of dessert. He marched her to the door, thrusting the dish into her hands. 'At least you've finished them in here.

Take them somewhere else and stop acting like a spoiled brat for once in your life.'

He pushed her through the door and closed it after her, coming back to the table and taking a long drink of wine before apologising very briefly and carrying on the discussion about tomorrow's work as though nothing had happened. Brie was appalled. She could see the muscles working in Adam's jaw and knew Susan had deserved a telling-off, but the way the two of them had erupted with each other so fast had shocked her. Susan was a child, but Brie considered Adam was mature enough to have acted with a bit more dignity.

Recalling her own reactions to Susan's antics on the plane though, she knew how easily the girl could produce the very worst in people. Besides, she felt so uncomfortable at the dinner-table now, she just wanted to finish her own dessert and get out of there. The talk was all about the series now, and she may as well not have existed at all. She was too upset about Claire's problem and Susan's unpredictable behaviour to care. As soon as she had finished, she got up and told the men she'd leave them to their discussion and take coffee in her room since she had some letters to write.

'Brie, I'm sorry,' Adam looked at her as if he saw her properly for the first time since early that evening.

'Don't apologise to me, please!' She didn't want that. 'Have a useful day tomorrow if I don't see you in the morning, and we'll try to get the barbecue organised.'

She couldn't get out of there fast enough. Even before she reached the door, Les was talking about casting and who they were to get for the leads in the series, and Brie knew she was forgotten. She leaned against the door for a moment. It was definitely a different world, she thought. And she wondered if it was a mistake for Adam to bring his TV crews here. This villa should be a place for him to relax. He probably needed that haven very badly at times, and to mix the two might not be a good thing. But she certainly wasn't going to be the one to tell him that!

She went to the kitchen and asked Juanita to bring her some coffee in her room. She had to write to Claire. She couldn't get it out of her mind. Later, she'd find Susan and see if she had calmed down. That was her job, but her first priority was to find the words to tell Claire what she had discovered. Poor Claire...Brie's generous heart went out to her at that moment...

Half an hour later, having drunk an entire pot of coffee on her balcony and with a small pile of screwed-up letters in her waste-bin, Brie knew it was impossible to disclose her news in a letter. The right words wouldn't come. Nor could she get the image of Claire's reaction out of her mind. Guessing at the pleasure in Claire's face when she saw her friend's writing on the envelope, and then opening the letter to read the unwelcome contents. She just couldn't do it, and neither could she let Claire go on in ignorance of Diablo/Bill's real nature. Brie hardly noticed how her phrasing of his name had changed from Bill/Diablo to Diablo/Bill! The dark side of the man was definitely uppermost in her mind now. And there was only one way she could break the news to Claire.

With shaking hands, she found the dialling code for England, and picked up the phone. She hadn't rehearsed the way she would tell Claire. If she tried to dress it up gently, it still wouldn't alter the fact that Claire's Bill was supposedly engaged to be married, and the sooner Claire was warned of it the better.

'Hello?' Claire's voice answered questioningly after a few minutes, as loud and clear as if she was standing beside Brie.

'Claire, it's me,' Brie heard the huskiness in her own voice. 'I—I thought this was better than writing a letter—'

'Brie, how wonderful! How is everything? Is the villa beautiful? Is the sun shining? We had the most awful downpour today. What's the terrible child like? I'm glad you phoned because I've got the most fabulous news to tell you, and it's been awful not to let on, but I knew you'd try and talk me out of it—' She giggled suddenly, and Brie realised she sounded more bubbly than usual. She felt a sudden foreboding, hearing a muted whispering at the other end of the line and unable to discern what it was.

'Claire, listen to me a minute—'

'I will, honestly, only Bill keeps trying to feed me champagne, and if I sound funny it's because I've had too much already—'

'Bill Jones? Diablo Hades, you mean? Is he there with you, Claire?' She knew she was sounding like a mother-hen, but warning bells were sounding loud and clear in her head. He hadn't taken long to move in, had he? Brie knew he'd been down in London for most of the past week, and that Claire had seen a lot of him in that time, but this was too much!

'Claire, listen, please—' she interrupted as her friend began giggling again. 'Adam's here at the villa—' she waited impatiently as Claire giggled even more shrilly. 'He's here with some technicians, and one of them said—well, I wish I didn't have to tell you like this—but he said that Diablo Hades is talking about getting married soon—'

'I know that!' Claire's giggles slowed down a little. 'Oh, Brie, I wanted to tell you myself, and now somebody's spoiled the surprise! And I wish you'd stop calling him Diablo Hades. Leave that to his fans. He's my Bill to me, and we're getting married at the end of next week by special licence. I wish you could be here, but it doesn't really matter, because Bill will have to be going on location with the TV people to oversee the script for his book, and he says Adam wants to do the filming on Corfu. So if it happens, I'll be coming with him, and we'll be spending our honeymoon on the island. How about that?'

Another voice broke in then, near to the receiver, while Brie was still taking in the shock of Claire's words.

'I promise you my intentions are honourable, Brie,' came Bill's teasing voice. 'I know it's all a bit sudden, but we had every reason for keeping it to ourselves for the time being, so that we wouldn't have people trying to talk us out of it!'

And that was directed right at herself, Brie thought! Claire spoke again while Brie was still stuck for words.

'You were always saying I was too timid, Brie, so you should be pleased that I'm changing all that! Say you're happy for me—'

'You know I am!' Brie found her voice at last. Relieved too, when she had thought she was breaking bad news to Claire! 'What about the job transfer to York then—?'

She heard Claire's happy laugh. 'Oh, the only books I'll be looking after in future are Bill's. I handed in my notice today, and once we're married I'm going to take on his manuscript-typing. Can you imagine it, Brie? All that lovely sci-fi stuff at first-hand—'

'That's all she's marrying me for,' Bill's teasing voice said into the phone, and from the brief pause at the other end, Brie could guess that Claire was making him very sure that wasn't all. The truth of it all still staggered her, but she couldn't be anything but happy for them both.

'Look, I'll give you this phone number, and you get in touch with me if you do come over here, won't you?' she said quickly. 'And many, many congratulations. Please keep in touch, Claire.'

By the time she put down the phone, she was starting to feel quite light-headed. Quiet, mousey little Claire had sounded so much in control of her life in a way she had never been before. In fact, Brie had often suspected that she got so much vicarious pleasure from her sci-fi reading and her library romances that she was content enough without the real-life variety.

And that was obviously going to be changed from now on! And Brie was the one urging Claire to 'keep in touch', the friend on the sidelines. It was an odd feeling, even though she was enormously pleased for Claire. And sudden or not, when Brie remembered the way Claire and Bill had looked at each other at the convention, with eyes for no-one else, it was obviously so right, so obviously love.

Relief flooded through her. There was no need to fret about Claire any more. So what was the other problem...? Brie remembered Susan with a stab of guilt. The poor girl must be hating being sent to her room so ignominiously. Feeling expansive now that she knew Claire wasn't being more or less jilted at the altar, Brie went out of her room to the wing where Susan had her bedroom and tapped on the door.

'Go away! I don't want to see anybody,' came Susan's belligerent voice.

'It's me, Susan. Would you like some coffee? I could ask for some to be sent up for us both. Why don't you come along to my room and have some with me?' She would be awash with coffee soon, but it was the only thing she could think of at that moment. Music blared out from a hi-fi in the girl's room, and after a moment she opened the door a crack, her face still sulky and suspiciously red-eyed.

'I don't like coffee. Pottsy and me have both had some tea. I sent down for it.'

'Can I come in a minute?' Brie said,

seeing the large dog sprawling across the bed in blissful ease.

'I suppose so,' Susan sulked. 'I'm not doing anything, only listening to music.'

'I was only curious to see your room, that's all,' Brie said lightly. 'You can tell a lot about a person by their room, their books and things.'

'And how untidy they are!' Susan sat down beside the dog, her arm around him and daring Brie to comment on the state of the bed, or the clothes strewn about. Why should she care? Juanita or someone else would pick them up tomorrow.

'I just think how lucky you are compared with what I had as a child, that's all. I lived in a small flat with my parents, and my room was little more than a cupboard. If I wasn't tidy in it, I couldn't get into bed. I'd have loved to throw my things about too.'

Susan stared at her suspiciously. 'Where are your parents now?'

'They live in Scotland. I don't see them all that often, but we keep in touch—'

'That's nice for you.'

The words might have been insolent, but for the way her fingers were suddenly clenching the dog's shaggy hair until her knuckles were taut. Brie felt compassion sweep over her.

'You miss your parents, don't you, Susan?' she said gently.

Susan's voice was brittle. 'They never missed me when they sent me away to school in England! I hardly saw them. You can't miss people you hardly ever saw, can you? I never even cried when they died in the boating accident. It didn't feel as if it happened to people that I knew. I never cry. My father said it was weakness to cry over things that couldn't be changed.' She spoke in a jerky fashion, unbelievably tense. Brie felt very sad for her.

'Oh Susan, it's not weakness to cry for the people you love,' she said at last. The girl rounded on her angrily.

'They didn't love me, did they? They wouldn't have sent me away if they loved me. Adam doesn't love me either, or he'd let me come home and go to school here. I hate having to go away all the time.'

She half-buried herself in the obliging Pottsy, face down on the bed, while Brie looked at her helplessly. Her moods swung so quickly from the sudden blaze of excitement downstairs to the depths of depression, and right now she was best left alone. Brie went out of the room quietly, closing the door behind her. When she turned, Adam was in the corridor, and she wondered just how long he had been there, just how much he had heard.

'I was looking for you,' he said abruptly. 'I'm sorry about the little fraças downstairs. It's an unfortunate habit in this house that dinner-parties often wind up that way. I apologise for my sister and myself.'

He hadn't heard a thing, Brie decided. She took the initiative.

'Adam, if you were going to give Susan a talking-to right now, could you leave it, please? She's upset—'

'Upset? She should think how she upsets other people by her tantrums,' he said angrily. He looked at Brie's flushed face. 'All right. If you'll come and have a drink with me in my study, I'll leave it for tonight. My people have gone down to the village to a taverna. We don't keep tabs on each other here. Come and join me, will you?'

She could hardly refuse. And in the comfortable male preserve, she sat in a large leather chair opposite him and told him of her phone call to England, without mentioning the panic that had made her call Claire.

'So it's your friend that Hades is marrying?' Adam said in surprise. 'The girl with the owl glasses who was sitting with you at breakfast? I remember.'

'It was Claire who asked me to go to the convention with her,' she reminded him. 'I wouldn't have known about it otherwise.'

Her gaze clashed with his. She hadn't gone there expressly to meet Adam Andrikos, the look said, and his grin told her he accepted it at last. He looked very much at home in the other leather chair, lazily sprawled out, his long legs stretching out towards hers. They looked very comfortable together, Brie thought uneasily, drinking wine, with the warm night scents drifting in through the windows, thrown open for the evening.

'I've a small apartment a bit farther up the coast. Do you think your friend would resent it if I offered her and Hades the use of it for their honeymoon? It would be convenient for me to have him near at hand for discussions, and you may like your friend's company now and then—when the two of them aren't otherwise engaged, of course.' He spoke in a slow lazy voice, watching her face. And Brie couldn't stop the pleasure in her voice as she answered.

'I think Claire would be delighted. It's very generous of you, Adam—'

'I've told you I can be very nice when I want to be. It's time you started believing it.' He lifted the wine bottle. 'Another drink—or bed?'

Brie felt her heart begin to pound. It had been quite an evening already without that awareness of the double meaning in his words. And this time she couldn't miss it. This time there was the unmistakable flicker of desire in Adam's eyes. He didn't really expect her to respond to such an audacious question, but she guessed he was just sounding her out. He probably needed to do little more than that with the women who were aspiring actresses, she thought suddenly. Wasn't that what he had suspected her of being from her application for the job as Susan's chaperone? She gave an amused little laugh as she put down her empty glass and got to her feet.

'I'll decline both invitations, thank you,' she looked him squarely in the eyes to let him know she knew exactly what he meant. 'Bed sounds very appealing to me right now. I'm so tired I'm ready to drop, so good-night, Adam. I'll see you tomorrow.'

If she thought he might have leapt up and tried to prolong the interlude, to pull her to his arms and kiss her, then she was mistaken. He did neither, merely stayed where he was and let her go. And that was the most frustrating thing about this entire, disruptive evening, starting with Susan's tantrums and the disturbance about Diablo Hades, who she had better start thinking about as Bill Jones from now on!...to the phone call with Claire, and her exhilarated news...then Susan's unknowing revelations about her own frustrations. Now Adam, whom Brie wanted to treat her like a woman, yet was too afraid to respond to his slightest move because her rating would go down. Frustration was the name of this particular game all right, Brie thought, suddenly as tense as Susan Andrikos, but for a very different reason.

# CHAPTER 7

Brie had fallen into Adam's silly game of giving him ratings. Ten out of ten for offering the apartment to Claire and Bill for their honeymoon. She couldn't fault the generous gesture. After all, he needn't have done it. And ten out of ten for not exploiting the offer by putting conditions on it as far as Brie was concerned. It surprised her a little. Adam's reputation was such that she had more than half expected it, but apart from that brief flare of desire she'd seen in his eyes and the suggestion of another drink or bed, he'd merely let her go.

He could act the gentleman, she admitted. He could also irritate her. If he really cared about her, he would have been more persistent...but of course, he didn't care. She kept reminding herself of it. While Brie...she wasn't sure how she felt now. She wished he hadn't come to Corfu while she was there. She wished he didn't keep popping up at unexpected times, making her heart beat twice as fast as normal. She wished he wouldn't suddenly give her those long penetrating looks that seemed to see right through her, into those innermost thoughts she didn't yet understand herself.

She didn't see him next morning. He and his TV people were gone early, and the tutor, Miss Vesey, arrived right after breakfast, while Susan was still grumbling about having to do lessons when she was on vacation. So Brie had the morning to herself, and wandered away from the villa to the tiny village a mile or so away.

The island was less commercialised in this area, the tourists keeping nearer to the holiday towns and coasts. There was a marvellous sense of freedom about it, the warm breeze scented by the ocean and the wild flowers. It was a paradise for lovers, and Claire and Bill would love it here.

Brie felt suddenly very alone. Normally she enjoyed the feeling of being alone with the elements. It was exhilarating, yet today a feeling almost akin to depression was alternating with her pleasure. It was crazy. She had always liked that feeling of being alone in the world on occasions, but not today. Today she wanted a tall male body to be walking beside her, matching stride for stride, compatible in every way.

The thoughts skidded through her head, unable to be silenced. She missed him. She missed the elegant loping walk he had. She missed the way he turned towards her and his dark eyes sparkled out a message. She missed his voice...especially his voice. It was deep and rich and could turn her knees to water. It could make her angrier in seconds than she had ever been. It could make her melt inside...

A sea-bird cried above her head, making her jump, and Brie knew it wasn't only that that was making her heart pound more quickly. It was thoughts of Adam. Ever since their first meeting she had thought of him so much, almost constantly, that the brief span of time she had known him hardly mattered. She had always known him. He was as necessary to her as breathing, and she was falling in love with him...

'I can't,' she whispered aloud, knowing there was no-one else to hear. 'It would be the biggest mistake of my life to fall for a man like Adam Andrikos. There's no future in it—'

She stopped, a thickness in her throat as

she swallowed. Her throat ached with the realisation of it all. There was no future for her and Adam because of the man he was, a perpetual bachelor, according to the media, the man about town with a beautiful woman on his arm like another accessory, and just as interchangeable. While Brie...Brie was the kind of woman who needed an exclusive kind of love, a once-in-a-lifetime orange-blossom kind of love that went with total commitment and a wedding ring, and a happy-ever-after promise...the two of them were as unlike as chalk and cheese.

If she were to settle for a brief affair, of course...she wasn't even sure if Adam would go along with that. And she certainly wouldn't, she added hastily to herself. She was forced to admit that there was at least a sense of family duty in him to care what sort of woman took on Susan's chaperoning, even if his methods were unorthodox, Brie still couldn't be certain if he had made the brief passes at her because he liked her for herself, or because of his ridiculous test. It piqued her, even more now that she was honest about her own feelings at last. She loved him. She tried out the words in her mind. She loved him. She loved Adam Andrikos...they seemed to soar in her head in a sudden fever of excitement at the knowledge, until a small gust of cool wind that whipped her hair about her face brought her back to earth. A fat lot of good it would do her to love him. It would only make things more difficult, and she had to be glad that he would be going back to London tomorrow. Glad...and frustrated.

The walk to the village was quickly accomplished, and Brie made herself take an interest in the bright umbrellas outside the cafes and tavernas, the huge fresh fruit displayed outside the shops, the lazy way of life that was so attractive. She bought a cold drink at one of the cafes and watched the small boats out in the bay, the heat haze over the water making it dance and glitter in the strong sunlight. After a while, that palled, and Brie went back to the villa. It was nearly lunch-time, and Susan had finished the day's lessons, and was in a foul mood.

'Miss Vesey did nothing but tell me what a waste of time it is to try and teach me anything. Why does she bother? I don't want her here. Why can't I go to the school here instead of being sent away—?'

'Don't you ever get tired of playing the same old record?' Brie asked her. 'I've heard that a dozen times already, and it's not going to change anything, Susan. Why not try and do as your brother wants and make everybody happy?'

Susan glared at her. 'Is that what you do? I saw the way he was looking at you last night. He fancies you, doesn't he?'

Brie felt her face grow hot, and didn't miss the resentment in the question. She tried to keep her temper, remembering the plaintive way Susan had said so flatly that her brother didn't love *her*.

'I'm just here to do a job, and you know that, Susan. It could be much more pleasant for both of us if we tried to like each other. And you're just being plain stupid to think your brother doesn't care about you. He's a very caring person really.'

She didn't know why she was defending him, nor why she insisted that he was caring. At first she had truly believed Adam cared about no-one but himself. She didn't think that was the case now.

'He's brought other women here, you know,' Susan was trying to goad her into anger again. 'Beautiful women, models and actresses and so on. They all adore him, and he could have any woman he wanted—'

'Then you don't really have to worry about me, do you?' Brie said evenly. 'I'm just a paid employee, and I don't adore him.'

Not in the besotted, meaningless way that Susan intimated, Brie amended silently. She had felt a new pang as Susan reeled off the kind of women Adam had brought here in the past, and gave a mental shrug. If she couldn't compete, it hardly mattered. The less she thought about herself and Adam the better, knowing how futile it was.

'You don't like me, do you?' Susan said now, watching the changing expressions on Brie's face and interpreting them in her own way.

Brie knew she had to go carefully. Susan wasn't a girl to be gushed over, and she would recognise false platitudes in a minute. She would have had plenty of those in her short life, from women wanting to impress Adam, Brie guessed.

'I could like you a lot,' she said truthfully. 'I think you're a gutsy girl with plenty of character, and I admire that. I know you're capable of affection from the way you love that crazy dog of yours, and it's a pity you can't extend that affection to people.'

'Well, thanks for the pep talk.' She paused. 'Do you really admire my character?'

'Some of it,' Brie grinned. 'I think you've got plenty of it, I said, which isn't quite the same thing. It's a case of when you're good, you're probably very very good, but when you're bad—'

'I know. I'm horrid.' This time, Susan's face broke into an answering grin. 'How would you like a nursemaid at fourteen years old?'

'You're not fourteen yet, and I wouldn't like it at all. But I'm nobody's nursemaid, just your friend. I'll strike a bargain with you. I'll be your friend for today, if you'll be mine. Just for today. We'll let tomorrow take care of itself. What do you say?'

It had worked with some of the small children Brie had cared for. They had been intrigued by the idea, and the tomorrows had always been sunny. She wouldn't guarantee anything like that with Susan Andrikos, but to her relief, the girl nodded slowly.

'O.K. Today we're friends. When's lunch? I'm starving.'

Brie laughed, and the atmosphere was lighter than it had been since their arrival. Susan could be very likeable when she got rid of the great chip on her shoulder, and the afternoon was spent very amicably on the beach, with the dog going wild in the rolling waves and shaking himself all over them to their screams of laughter. Susan was a different girl, Brie thought in amazement. It wouldn't last, of course. She knew that.

They had helped Juanita get the barbecue ready for the evening. Miguel had taken the containers down to the beach before the men got back from their trip to the mountains, and it was all set up and ready.

'We'll have to wear our old things,' Susan said. 'Adam's hopeless at cooking really, and makes a terrible smoke with the steaks and sausages. You'll be covered in black bits in no time.'

Brie didn't have anything very old with her, and made do with a tee shirt and shorts over her swimsuit, since Susan insisted they wear them, and that they'd be glad of a swim later to rid themselves of Adam's cooking smells. It all sounded intimate and domesticated, and a world away from the high-tycoon life of a top TV producer in London. It endeared him to Brie, and also made her realise just how much Susan must miss this kind of life, second nature to her, when she was back in her strict boarding-school atmosphere in England. It did seem a shame...but it wasn't Brie's place to suggest that the girl had a point in not wanting to stay there. If she wasn't academically bright, as Brie suspected, then no wonder she was unhappy being with other girls smarter than she was, and no wonder she hit out in the only way she knew, by being thoroughly objectionable!

A beach barbecue, Andrikos-style, was pretty sophisticated, Brie discovered. An insulated cold-box was part of the baggage taken down the lane by the obliging Miguel, and contained chilled fruit and cream in individual plastic dishes, and bottles of champagne. Another cold box held the steaks and sausages, while in a third were ready-prepared salad rolls to accompany them.

Adam and his TV people got back around five-thirty, dusty and dishevilled, but fired with enthusiasm as they flopped unceremoniously on elegant chairs in the villa's lounge and gratefully drank the cold drinks Juanita brought them. Susan perched on the edge of Adam's chair, and Brie thought fleetingly that she wished she had the right to do the same. Instead, she sat near the window, listening to the talk flow between the men.

'It's perfect, Adam,' Les was saying through his cigar-smoke. '*Planet* might have been written with exactly that location in mind. The tiny chapels perched on the mountain-sides are just right for the *Hail to the Darkness* sequence, and the caves perfect for the *Weird Demon* scene. Couldn't be better. I'll run off some sketches as soon as I get back to London tomorrow—'

'If Hades wants to start on the script himself, I suggest we get a good script-writer of our own on it at the same time and mix the two if we have to,' David said. 'There are some pretty impossible stunts in the novel, and we may well have to temper them down a little.'

'It'll all be taken care of,' Adam agreed. 'The main thing is that we four are agreed, then we can take it farther, director, costings, and so on. We're all agreed it's a viable proposition, are we?'

Brie found she was holding her breath.

She wanted Adam's project to be a success. He'd be working here...and by the time it happened, she would probably be back in England looking for the next job. She looked down at her hands in her lap, wishing things could be different. She heard the men agree enthusiastically.

'When will you be here, Adam?' Susan demanded to know. 'Before I have to go back to that rotten school?'

Adam laughed, patting her knee affectionately and not riling for once.

'We aim to start prelims pretty soon, but I'm not promising anything yet. But I think you'll be seeing me around quite a lot in the next few weeks.'

Susan gave a squeal of joy, and Brie looked up in time to see Adam watching her steadily. Wondering what her reaction would be, she thought immediately. She hardly knew. Joy flooded through her too, though she wasn't sure how clever it was going to be for her to see the man she loved in close proximity for the next few weeks.

'Does that mean you won't be needing me so long?' she said quickly. 'If you're here on the island—'

'I shall still need you, Brie,' Adam said.

'We made a contract, didn't we? Your job is still safe, don't worry.'

She wished he needed her, *really* needed her. The thought was so strong in her head, the desire so passionate, she was afraid he must see it all in her eyes, and she got to her feet at once.

'We'd better go and get ready, Susan, and leave these people to their discussion.' As she saw Susan's lower lip jut out rebelliously, Brie caught at her hand as she passed the chair. 'Come on, *friend!*'

Susan grinned and responded. Brie saw the amazement on Adam's face as they went out giggling together, and felt an absurd little glow of pleasure that she had been able to handle Susan in however small a degree, when there were times when Adam himself clearly found her impossible.

The two of them went upstairs and separated. Brie wanted a shower, despite the fact that she'd probably be covered in black specks before the barbecue was over. She was hot and tacky from the day in the sun, and her skin was already deepening into a golden tan. That was definitely one of the perks of the job, she thought. She went into her bathroom and stripped off her clothes, and let the blissfully warm water run over her body, shaking it through her hair in as much ecstacy as Pottsy down at the beach. The Corfu air was hot, but she could learn to live with it, she told herself with a smile as she stepped out of the shower and wrapped a huge bath towel around herself.

She rubbed herself dry enough to slip into her swimsuit, and then sat out on her balcony in a lounger to let her hair dry naturally into soft curls all over her head. Claire used to say it made her look like a cherub, which was probably an apt simile for Adam's angel of the evening...the little phrase leapt into her mind. She had hated it then, but its appeal had subtly changed. She closed her eyes against the glare of the sun and let the memory of that night at the convention drift into her mind.

The convention, and meeting Adam...the stroll along the promenade and realising that she was no longer alone...the moment when he had pulled her into his arms and kissed her, as passionately as though he had really meant it. She had tasted his skin, breathed in his scent, loved him even then, without really being aware of it. And the spell had been broken abruptly enough by his prosaic remarks when she had fought against him.

Ten out of ten was the mark Brie gave herself at that instant, for not allowing her feelings to show, for not admitting that sane and sensible Brie Roberts could fall in love at first sight like any other woman...

'Be careful of your English skin, angel,' she heard a soft voice say, very close to her.

So close that the voice seemed to be in her own head, deep and rich and sensual. Adam's voice. She turned quickly, aware of the uneven beat of her heart. He stood on the adjoining balcony to hers, shirt open to the waist, preparing to take his own shower. Brie could see the hair-roughened chest, against which a gold medallion gleamed in the sunlight. She rammed her dark glasses on to her face, and as she did so, Adam leaned over and gently took them off again, before stepping easily over the dividing rail between them.

Before she realised what he was going to do, he had crouched beside her so that his face was level with hers as she lazed back on the sun lounger. His face was close to hers. She could see the gold flecks in the darkness of his eyes. She could breathe the faintly odorous scent of him, masculine and subtle after his long day in the mountains, and unexpectedly exciting to her senses.

'Why are you always so afraid of looking at me, Brie?' Why do you deny me the pleasure of looking into those beautiful eyes?' He asked her softly, his voice an intimate caress.

A sudden sharp urge to weep took Brie by surprise at the gentleness in him. It was sweet torture to have him so close to her like this, and know that his words meant less than nothing. Knowing that they were part of the pattern, meaningless, and said for one purpose only. He couldn't believe she could go on resisting him. She knew instinctively that he would go on pursuing her if only for that one reason. And that once she succumbed, she'd probably be out of a job!

Not that the job was important any more. Brie realised it in a flash. The job itself meant nothing. Adam himself did—and so did Susan. Little madam she may be, but she was beginning to get under Brie's skin. It was hard enough being on the brink of growing up, without being bereft of parents and imagining yourself to be cast aside and totally unloved. Brie's irritation with the girl was dissipating fast. In its place an enormous sympathy was growing. She swallowed as discreetly as she could, and gave Adam an unwavering look.

'I'm not afraid of looking at you, Adam. Unless it sometimes appears that way because I don't want to reveal my disapproval of your handling of Susan—'

'We weren't talking about Susan.' He wasn't going to let her get away with that, and the glint in his eyes told her he knew exactly what she was doing. He inched closer, his hands reaching out and closing over her bare arms. She was still slightly damp after her shower, and she could feel the heat of his skin on hers. She tried desperately to think of something bright and witty to say, to lessen the suddenly supercharged atmosphere between them. The words came out thickly, and not at all in the way or format she intended.

'Adam, please don't.' They were a whispered plea. 'I don't want my rating to go down—'

'Damn your rating,' he voice was as thick as hers. 'Forget that ridiculous statement for one minute, can't you? Just believe me when I tell you I want to hold you in my arms and kiss you at this moment more than I've wanted anything in my life before. You know the way the war games are played, when both sides call a truce at Christmas and fraternise? Let's have Christmas in July, my beautiful angel—'

His hands slid upwards, caressing her shoulders and pulling her closer, and if he turned on her immediately afterwards, then Brie didn't care. The need to be in his arms was so intense, so exquisitely urgent, that she gave a soft sigh of pure pleasure and melted against him as his mouth crushed against hers. She was caught to his chest, the thin fabric of her swimsuit the only thing separating their bodies. It might have been nothing...

It might have been seconds or hours that she remained a part of him. Time lost its meaning as the sweet rapture of the kiss swept through her. For these moments at least, he was totally hers, and nothing could take that away from her. Her arms closed around his powerful back, hardly noticing how naturally they moved there, nor how hungrily she matched his kiss.

A sudden shrieking from below the balconies made Adam draw reluctantly away from her as Susan played with a deliriously barking Pottsy. He stared into Brie's face for a moment, his eyes expressionless, his large hand cupping her chin and refusing to let her turn away this time.

'So my angel's not quite as immune as she pretends to be,' Adam said gently. 'I'm glad. I see enough robot women in my job, from harridans in the crew to those formidable actresses who'd kill one another for a coveted part. Thank God for a real woman!'

Brie ran her tongue around her lips. Lips that Adam had just kissed. Was he sincere? He certainly sounded it. She felt a burning need for him to say more. To say he'd fallen as madly in love with her as she had with him. Even if it was a lie, at that moment she needed that knowledge, ached for it. She needed him.

He touched his finger to her mouth, tracing its soft outline. Then his finger began a long sensual trail around her cheek and throat, down the pulsing line of it to the creamy swell of her breasts. His hand rested gently above the left one.

'Does your heart always beat so fast? Or have I broken through that efficient outer layer at last?' His voice was seductive.

Aware that Susan and Pottsy were right below the balcony, Brie managed a small laugh, knowing full well that her erratic heartbeats were due to one reason only.

'There's not much of an outer layer there!' She deliberately misunderstood him, reaching for his hand and removing it. Adam caught at her fingers, surely feeling the tremor in them, Brie thought. He turned her hand palm upwards, capturing it and placing it to his lips. The small gesture, so absurdly old-fashioned and gallant, had the power to stir her.

'Later, we'll swim in the sea,' he murmured. 'No-one will see us, and I promise you an experience you won't forget. After the barbecue, Brie.'

He turned and vaulted back over the balcony rail while she was still taking in his words. She recalled the words he'd said earlier. Bathing at mid-night...and knew at once that this was what he meant. The two of them, bathing naked in total seclusion...

The outrage she expected to feel didn't come, and instead there was a fast-growing exhilaration inside her. If she was living dangerously, recklessly, she didn't care.

For once, she was going to live life in the fast lane.

The evening was both a delight and interminably long, because to Brie it had only one ending, and that was the time she would be alone with Adam. Her thinking was helped by the unreal sensations evoked by drinking champagne on the beach, and the magic of the ocean and the atmosphere, a million miles removed from any normal kind of life. Corfu was an enchanted place to Brie that night.

And it was Adam himself who furthered the euphoric feeling. He seemed so carefree here, so different from the tycoon image he normally wore so dynamically. So sweet to Susan, who responded more naturally than Brie would have believed possible. Couldn't he see it? She wondered briefly. All the girl needed was a little love and attention. It was all any of them needed...

After the marvellous swim in that still warm and silken water, they donned towelling robes and ate Adam's succulent steaks and drank the wine until the night's hues deepened. The horizon gradually merged with the blue of the sea, and the enormous yellow moon threw golden kaleidoscopic patterns on the ever-changing water. It was so beautiful it almost made Brie want to cry, the way powerful music or deeply emotional poetry reached the senses. And all the time she knew that all this was only a prelude...a waiting game.

The technicians were ready to call a halt long before mid-night. Their day in the mountains had all but finished them, Les groaned. Susan too, was ready by then to go back to the villa with everyone else. It was only when they parted for their own rooms at the villa that Adam caught Brie's hand for a moment. Under cover of the laughter from the others, he spoke softly so that only she could hear.

'Meet me here in ten minutes, angel,' he said.

Before she could say anything, he had clapped a hand on Stanley's thin shoulder and asked how soon he'd be able to see proofs of the day's still shots.

'After lunch tomorrow, I'd say, Adam. We'll be leaving early, won't we?'

Brie didn't hear his reply. She'd forgotten until that moment that Adam would be leaving tomorrow. Somehow tonight had seemed like a beginning, not an ending. Reality was rushing towards her very fast. If she had any sense, she'd go straight to bed, and then she'd have nothing to regret...and nothing to remember, either. She pushed aside the nagging little voice of warning in her head. Her job was necessarily a responsible one, caring for other peoples' children. Just for once, she was going to be as reckless as she wanted to be...

Adam was already waiting for her when she went back downstairs, stealthily, feeling like a conspirator. They both still wore the towelling robes, but beneath hers, Brie had exchanged her swimsuit for a brief bikini. She didn't try to guess what he wore beneath his. He caught at her hand and they retraced their steps to the beach, and neither of them spoke. Words would have been superfluous, Brie thought with a catch in her throat, thinking how extraordinarily sensitive he was to realise it as much as she did.

The magic of their surroundings was enough. It was a scenario for lovers, the huge yellow moon and the warm dappled sea, the soft sand and the scented breezes. And the two of them, alone in a world that belonged only to them.

'Share the ocean with me, angel,' Adam said softly.

She looked at him mutely. His dark hair was ruffled by the breeze, making him look oddly young for a moment. But there was nothing immature about that powerful physique as he slowly untied the belt of his robe and let it drop to the sand. He was like a Greek god, standing motionless for a moment. She felt the urge to touch him to see if he was real, only she dare not. Once she did, he would surely know the depth of her feelings for him.

She felt him loosen the tie of her robe, and the warm breeze caressed her skin where the tiny scraps of fabric began and ended. Adam palmed her midriff in a gentle movement, lightly fingering the thin material of her bikini.

'Try it without,' he said. 'Once you've swum naked in the ocean, even these bits of material will seem like straitjackets afterwards, I promise you.'

Without waiting, he turned and walked away from her, into the enveloping waves. Brie hesitated, then dropped her own robe with shaking hands, taking only seconds to slip out of the two pieces of cloth before she ran to join him.

The water was incredibly warm, the sensation of it against her flesh more sensual than she had ever expected it to be. The sense of freedom was immense, the sense of oneness with God and creation a startling bonus to everything else. She was at once a sea creature, a mermaid, a minuscule atom in the vastness of time. She was a woman in a man's arms...

'Didn't I tell you how wonderful it would be?' Adam's voice was close to her cheek. She could feel the vibrato of it from somewhere deep in his chest that was crushing her breasts to his body. She was entangled in his limbs, entwined with him, part of him, her long golden hair floating on the surface of the water like mermaid strands. And she couldn't deny the magic of it all.

'I believe you!' She whispered as though unwilling to break the spell. Her eyes closed for a moment. 'Oh Adam, I feel—'

'What?' There was laughter in his voice now as his hold tightened, and his voice became wickedly teasing. 'Tell me what you feel, angel.'

'Don't you know?' Brie's eyes widened in feigned innocence. 'It was you who told me I'd never feel the same again after this experience—or words to that effect.'

'What experience?' He was persistent,

and she was aware that the little pulsating movements against her body were becoming more demanding. It was impossible to ignore them, nor to pretend that her own body wasn't responding to his, whether she wanted it to or not. And she did want it, so much. She wanted him with a fierceness that overwhelmed her.

'Adam, please don't tease me,' she mumbled against the salt taste of his shoulder. 'Don't—pretend with me, please. If this is all a game to you—'

He tipped up her chin, his gaze taking in the soft tremble of her mouth and the droplets of water sparkling like diamonds on her lashes. From the ocean—or something else? Adam reacted in a way that surprised himself at that moment. She was his for the taking, and he sensed it unquestioningly. He knew her almost as intimately in those moments as if he made love to her, yet there was something about her that halted his passion. He released her from the powerful hold he had on her and the water between them seemed ocean-deep to Brie.

She heard him laugh again, a small, brittle sound in the silence of the night.

'Of course it's a game. I thought we

both knew that. All life's a game, isn't it? I thought that's what we agreed on, angel. A war game, Christmas in July—'

Brie shivered, even though the night was still warm. But it had all gone cold on her. Tomorrow she may be glad that she hadn't done something irrevocable, but that was tomorrow. All she could feel now was an enormous frustration and anger. A game, she thought bitterly. That's all this was to him, until she'd lowered her guard and let him see how much she was affected by him by her thoughtless remark. She swallowed, tasting the acidity of sea-water, and gathered up her pride.

'I'm thankful I won't be around until New Year then,' she said tautly, and struck out for the beach in long sweeping strokes. She ran across the sand, struggling into her robe as though she couldn't bear him to see her body a second longer. Exposed to him in every way, she felt vulnerable and young, and more like weeping than she ever had in her life before. While Adam was still pulling his robe around him and telling her to wait for him, she was running back through the lane to the villa, and the sanctuary of her own room.

# CHAPTER 8

Brie was conscious of a feeling of being trapped, by her own feelings, and by being here in a job that was causing her more emotional upheaval than satisfaction. She was trapped on this idyllic island when she would dearly have loved to be at Claire's wedding—or anywhere else for that matter, that didn't evoke memories of Adam Andrikos.

But wherever she went, she knew she couldn't escape her own thoughts and longings. It was all futile, because all this was a game to him. Before she'd reached the villa last night, he'd finally caught up with her. To her heightened nerves, his grip on her arm was cruelly sharp, his voice harsh.

'Brie, I make it a policy never to mix business with pleasure, and I hate breaking my own rules. It's a form of weakness—'

'I'm sorry if I forced you into doing anything so—so human!' She whipped back at him, oozing with sarcasm. 'Let's just forget it, shall we? It never happened. As far as I'm concerned, that's the way I want it.'

She pushed past him then, knowing she wouldn't forget, nor ever could. The humiliation of his apology made things even worse. But he hadn't apologised, she raged later. It was she who'd said she was sorry, and she hated him for goading her into doing so. She hated him, she told herself, over and over.

In the morning, he was gone. Brie awoke with a headache caused by tension and a sleepless night, and was thankful that Susan seemed in a reasonably amicable mood. Apparently she had got up very early and seen the men leave the villa.

'He's getting Helen Churchill to do the script-writing for the new series,' Susan announced excitedly. 'There was a message for him on his answering machine last night to say she'd do it, and she'd see him in London with the writer. She's fantastic, and crazy about Adam, of course. I think he's crazy about her too. He always used to be, and now they'll be working together again, well, anything can happen, can't it?'

She watched Brie closely to see the effect of her words. Brie thought her blatantly transparent and was tempted to snap back that it didn't matter a damn to her who Adam was crazy about or who he worked with, but she bit back the words, knowing Susan would enjoy such an outburst. Maybe it didn't matter about mixing business and pleasure when the two concerned were involved in the same project, Brie thought with an unwanted wave of misery. But hadn't she thought she and Adam were also involved in project Susan...?

'Good,' she said coolly. 'I hope they'll be very happy together.'

Susan glared at her. 'Don't you care? I mean, after those pictures in the papers, and that TV programme?'

'Didn't I tell you not to believe everything you see? When you're a bit older, you'll learn the truth in that, Susan.'

She saw the mutinous look come into the girl's eyes.

'Well, if all grown-ups tell lies and just invent things for good newspaper stories and TV pictures, I don't see any point in being told to tell the truth if you just have to forget it all. I don't think I'm interested in being grown-up if people can't be honest with each other.'

Brie gave her a rueful smile. 'Sometimes you're more grown-up than the rest of us, darling,' she said without thinking. She glanced at her watch. 'Isn't it time you reported to Miss Vesey?'

Susan looked at her oddly. 'You called me darling. Are we friends again today then? Two days running? It must be a record.'

Brie laughed, touched at the almost desperate plea in Susan's voice that she obviously didn't realise she was revealing. 'We're friends for as long as you like.'

Susan pretended to back off. 'Oh no. One day at a time, please! Don't let's overdo it!'

She went out, grinning, as relaxed as any other child her age, and Brie allowed herself a moment's pleasure that she at last seemed to have struck a chord with Susan. The pleasure dimmed a little, wishing it could be that way for her and Adam. And tormented by a sudden jealousy as she thought of the unknown Helen Churchill who was apparently crazy about him, and would by now be all set to meet him in London. She'd be coming here too, presumably, Brie thought suddenly, and how was she going to feel then?

Maybe it was for the best. To see Adam Andrikos in action with some sophisticated TV script-writer would let Brie see how utterly foolish it was to think he could ever fall in love with his sister's chaperone! She kept telling herself as much, and refused to admit how lonely the days were without him at the villa. There were many times when they clashed, when the tension between them seemed unbearable, but there were other times Brie remembered too. Like the time they had sat so companionably in Adan's den and discussed Susan, and the sweet domesticity of it had touched her heart. She had known him for such a short time, and yet it seemed as if she had always known him. In that short time, there was already too much to forget.

She tried to push him out of her mind and to think of other things. Claire. Claire, who was marrying her Bill at the end of next week and would be coming here to Corfu afterwards while Bill worked on the series with Adam and Helen Churchill and the TV people. Brie felt an enormous rush of pleasure knowing Claire would be here, as though she was her one ally in a world that had suddenly been knocked sideways for her. Claire would understand her feelings...

Even as she thought it, Brie knew how totally unfair it would be for her to confide her unhappiness to Claire, who shouldn't have any small clouds to dim her horizon on her honeymoon! And even afterwards, when it would be so great to enjoy each other's company while Bill was working, Brie still couldn't spoil Claire's time here by confessing she was stupid enough to fall for a man like Adam Andrikos. Particularly, the little spark of self-pride reminded her, since Claire had been so sure it was exactly what would happen!

Adam phoned several times during the next week, ostensibly to speak to Susan, who was clearly delighted he'd taken the trouble. And always asking to speak to Brie too, in that oddly stilted manner he'd developed with her since the night at the beach.

'Just checking,' he told her each time. 'I don't want you to think I neglect my responsibilities towards my sister, despite my unorthodox methods of arranging things. Is everything going smoothly?'

'Of course. I'm quite experienced in dealing with children, you know.' She dared him to respond to her use of that particular word, but he didn't. But then he obviously knew she wasn't experienced in love, Brie thought, crushed, or she'd have been able to handle that situation at the beach without going all cow-eyed on him. She was ruthless in her self-condemnation.

'Good.' Adam said briefly. 'That's what I counted on when I hired you. I've every confidence in you, Brie. Not everyone lasts the course where Susan's concerned.'

'Ten out of ten for effort?' she asked lightly. She heard him laugh, and for a second it was the same warm sound she remembered. Her fingers gripped the telephone cord more tightly.

'Ten out of ten for everything,' he drawled, and then the line went dead.

Brie put the receiver down slowly, wishing his voice didn't have the power to make her heart leap every time she heard it. Wishing he loved her. Wishing, wishing...

The phone rang for her again that evening. It was Claire.

'Brie, I'm so excited. Bill asked Adam it he'd be one of our witnesses, and he's agreed to it. And to think I never even knew him until such a little while ago. But that's not the best bit of news!'

Brie waited, just able to get a word in now and then.

'Adam agreed, and then asked if it wouldn't be nice for me if my best friend was a witness too. And that means you, of course! Adam's flying to Corfu the day before the wedding and bringing you to London with him, and then we'll all fly back together after we've had a meal at some swish club that Adam belongs to. He's putting it all on, Brie. Isn't he fabulous? He says it's his wedding present to us. I can hardly believe it's all happening!'

Neither could Brie. It stunned her for a minute. Here she'd been expecting to miss Claire's wedding, and not only was she to be a part of it, but Adam had seen to it that they were a cosy little foursome. He'd arranged everything without even consulting her. Of course, he was in London, but there were phones, weren't there? He'd said nothing at all earlier that evening. She forced the right amount of enthusiasm into her voice.

'Claire, that's wonderful. I was so sad at the thought of missing your big day. When was all this arranged, for heaven's sake?'

'Right this minute! Adam's here now—' There was muttering in the background, and then Claire's voice spoke excitedly again. 'Hold on, Brie, he wants to speak to you himself.'

She couldn't escape him. And this time his voice was full of a warm inflexion, presumably for the benefit of the other two, Claire and Bill.

'I know what you're going to say—that you've nothing to wear and I shouldn't have sprung it on you like this,' he said laughingly, just as though they were on very intimate terms. Even though it would be only Bill and Claire who were listening, Brie felt her hackles rise. He had a knack of taking people over just when he thought he would, but for Claire's sake there was nothing she could do about it. It was what she wanted—she just wished it hadn't been all-powerful Adam Andrikos who had arranged it so neatly.

'You're right, she snapped. 'And if you were going to say I can come as I am, forget it.'

She pulled her robe around her, just as though he could see that she'd just got out of the shower, and was naked beneath the towelling garment. How sensitive she was becoming to him, she thought angrily.

He laughed again, a sexy sound. 'I was thinking more of that gorgeous blue dress you wore on the night we met,' he went on. 'I haven't seen it since then, and it holds pleasant memories for me, and for you too, I hope. If you prefer to buy something new, ask Stavros to take you to the best boutique on the island and buy something ravishing. Charge it to my account, darling.'

Brie felt her cheeks burn. What must Claire and Bill be thinking of this conversation? Even if they were only hearing one side of it, Adam was making it plain that they were more than friends. Brie wouldn't have said they were even friends. Their relationship had gone far beyond that of employer and employee, and she still didn't know what he wanted of her. Lover? She'd thought so at the beach, when it had ended so abruptly. Then what?

'I'll pay for my own dress if I buy one,' she told him cuttingly. 'Can I speak to Claire again now, please?'

He didn't answer, and then Claire's voice was bubbling in her ear again, rattling out all the little details of her own dress, and repeating again and again how thrilled she was that Brie was going to be there on her big day. And Brie couldn't be so heartless as to quench her joy. She was terribly fond of Claire, and very happy for her. Finally she heard Claire say ruefully that they'd better stop talking for they'd have nothing left to say next week.

Brie felt exhausted when she hung up. Life had shifted direction again, and she was being thrust into a very romantic situation with Adam, whether she liked it or not. Witnesses at Claire and Bill's wedding...it was being kept a very small wedding, and a closely guarded secret from the press. Already Bill Jones, alias Diablo Hades, was newsworthy because of his books. Coupled with the tycoon producer, Adam Andrikos, and they have the newshounds on their necks in no time, and Claire wouldn't want her wedding turned into a circus.

For a minute on the phone, Brie had felt

tempted to suggest to Adam that Susan should attend as well. It would include his sister in his life...but then Brie decided against it. Susan was not part of Claire's life, and Brie saw no reason to bring any extra tension into Claire's wedding day by Susan's presence. There would be enough on her own account, she thought grimly, but for her friend's sake, it mustn't show. She and Adam must appear on perfectly good terms, whatever their inner feelings. And just what his were, she had no idea. She gave up fretting about it, and slid into bed, deciding that at the first opportunity, she'd ask Stavros to take her to the best boutique Adam mentioned. Juanita would know which one he meant. There was no way she was going to wear the blue dress she'd worn at the sci-fi convention!

By the time the day prior to the wedding arrived, Susan had been sulky because Brie was leaving the island with Adam, even though it was only for one night, and with the imperiousness of a girl who had always had everything money could buy, was openly venting her annoyance on everyone in sight.

Her resentment was only tempered by the arrival of some of the TV people for the preliminary shootings. They were staying at a hotel halfway between the villa and the mountain location that had practically been turned over to their use, and was fast becoming one of the tourist spots of the area, with several instantly-recognisable TV actors and actresses installed there. And Helen Churchill, the script-writer, had turned up at the villa a few days earlier to say hello to Susan and to Juanita. She was obviously used to coming here, Brie thought, with that sliver of jealousy again. Well-founded now that she saw how glamorous Helen really was. She was also nearer Adam's age than Brie's, sleek and sophisticated, and clever enough to treat Susan as an adult.

'So you're the girl in the newspaper photos,' Helen stated rather than asked, her gaze sweeping over Brie as though she couldn't quite see what all the fuss was about. Brie said that she was, lifting her chin a little higher and daring Helen to make anything of it.

'She's Adam's latest,' Susan chipped in with that irritating little sidelong glance at Brie.

'Don't be ridiculous, Susan,' Brie said with an exasperated sigh. 'You know exactly why I'm here—and remarks like that only prove that you need somebody around to keep an eye on you!'

Helen laughed easily, siding with Susan, and managing to put Brie into the fuddy-duddy brigade at once.

'I shouldn't worry about Susan, Brie—it is Brie, isn't it? She can look after herself perfectly well without a nanny, can't you, my darling? Come and tell me everything about that ghastly school of yours. Brie can amuse herself without us for the afternoon, I'm sure.'

She was dismissed as easily as if she didn't exist, Brie thought fuming. Thank goodness Helen wasn't staying at the villa, because she was sure they'd clash in no time, and not only on account of Adam Andrikos. Helen wasn't a type she particularly liked, though according to Juanita, she was warm-hearted and generous. You could have fooled her, Brie thought feelingly. Or maybe there was more than a touch of jealousy emanating from Helen too. It hadn't occurred to Brie before, but that remark about the newspaper photos was pretty forthcoming. Brie shrugged. Just as long as she didn't have to see much of Helen, they'd get along all right. And she didn't see the necessity for that to happen.

Brie pushed the woman out of her mind. Already she was getting excited at going to Claire's wedding. Going home. In her wardrobe there hung the new dress she'd bought at the boutique, finding ridiculous pleasure in paying for it herself. The dress was a pale lilac colour, filmy enough for summer evenings, and dressy enough for a wedding. It had bell-shaped sleeves and a full flowing skirt, and the neckline was deeply curved into a vee. She had called Claire and asked her to arrange for a corsage of toning flowers to be sent to the rooming house together with Claire's own bouquet.

Claire had decided on a calf-length chiffon dress trimmed with lace and petals, in white, of course. On her head, she was to wear a juliet cap also trimmed with pearls, and a wisp of a veil to her shoulders. Her flowers would be red roses. Claire was a traditionalist, despite the register office wedding. From the way Bill had swept her off her feet, it wouldn't have surprised Brie if Claire had agreed to be married in a tent! All the details had been relayed to Brie in the ecstatic phone call.

Brie checked her small suitcase on the day before the wedding. She didn't need to take much. The clothes she was wearing would do to travel back to Corfu again. She only needed the wedding outfit, together with the pale grey shoes and clutch bag and the pert little lilac hat that matched the dress exactly with its provocative hint of veiling. The wedding gift she'd bought for Claire and Bill needed careful packing, the beautiful deep blue tea-set decorated with real gold in a traditional Greek design. Brie gave a sudden sigh as she checked everything. How wonderful to be Claire right now. How wonderful to be so loved and cherished and to know that life was going to be happy ever after!

Adam arrived at lunchtime the day before the wedding. They hadn't expected him until later, and it gave Brie's heart a jolt when she saw him striding towards the villa in the easy way of his. Susan leapt to her feet and greeted him as noisily as the crazily jumping Pottsy. Susan had been irritable all day, picking on anything and everything to be objectionable, and straining Brie's patience to breaking point.

'Hey, what's all this?' Adam began to laugh as Susan burst into a stream of

Greek as he hugged her. 'I don't normally get such wild treatment—and speak in English, please. Don't you know it's rude to exclude Brie like this?'

He was teasing, and over Susan's head his eyes met Brie's. She wished she had the right to throw herself into his arms the way Susan did. For a moment the glow at seeing him so unexpectedly had sent the blood rushing to Brie's own cheeks, and now she could only stand there foolishly while Susan reverted to English.

'Why can't I come with you to this wedding, Adam? Why do I have to be left here on my own? I thought Brie was supposed to be my chaperone. I'll get up to everything bad while you're away, I promise you. Take me with you, *please!*'

Her words ended on a little squeal as Adam released her suddenly, his hands gripping her wrists in a vice-like hold. He gave her a none too gentle shake.

'You'll behave yourself and do exactly as Juanita tells you, miss,' he snapped, all the welcoming laughter gone in an instant. He glared at his sister just as she was glaring at him. To Brie it would have been comical if she hadn't sensed the frustration behind both of them. When Susan's unpredictable temper was let loose, Adam hadn't the faintest idea of how to deal with her. And Brie didn't feel the least inclination to intervene. For once, they could sort this out for themselves.

'Do you understand me?' Adam demanded as she stood in a sullen stance. 'You cannot come to London at this time. We shall be back tomorrow night, and you'll hardly have time to miss us. Added to which, you hate weddings, or so you've always told me, so what's so special about this one, except that Brie and I are going?'

That was the sole reason, Brie saw instantly. Why couldn't Adam see it too? It was excluding *Susan*, and she just couldn't bear that. She felt alone again. It was a similar feeling to when her parents died, Brie guessed. A hundred times less harrowing, but similar all the same. She tried to speak to Adam.

'Couldn't she—'

He turned on her. 'I've said all I want to say on the subject, Brie. Susan stays here. I won't have her spoiling Claire's day. She has the knack of ruining the most pleasant of occasions when she chooses.'

'I hate you!' Susan suddenly screamed

at him, beating her small fists against his implacable chest. 'You're a pig, and I hate you. I didn't want to go to your rotten old wedding anyway. I wish you'd stay in London and never come back.'

She rushed from him and into the villa, with Pottsy leaping at her heels in bewilderment. Brie felt limp. Five minutes ago it had been relatively peaceful, and she and Susan had been sitting in comparative companionship in the terraced garden. Now, everything had changed. Adam sat down heavily on the chair Susan had vacated. His hands were clenched into tight fists.

'You see what her tantrums are like?' He said angrily. 'She's impossible. I'm wondering if she should see a psychiatrist.'

'Adam—have you ever talked with her—about your parents' deaths?' Brie asked tentatively.

He snorted. 'She won't talk about them. She's as cold as ice when it comes to feeling any pain about what happened. Our father was the same. He could switch off his emotions whenever he chose.'

'I'd hardly say Susan was switching off just now!' Brie exclaimed.

'She didn't cry, did she? Normal kids

would cry, but not her. She's too hard for something so normal!'

'But have *you* tried talking with her about your parents? Just the two of you together, sharing your grief.' Brie persisted, knowing she was on dangerous delicate ground. Adam wasn't a man who cared to be told what to do, any more than his precocious sister did. In that, they were very alike.

'No,' he said shortly. 'Grief is a private thing.'

'You're wrong, Adam,' Brie said softly. 'Grief needs to be expressed somehow, whether in words or tears. If Susan can't do one, and you're denying her the need to do the other, then she's in danger of becoming introverted, despite all the tantrums. She lost the two people she must have loved best in the world, and now she only has you. How can you be so insensitive about her?'

'Is the lecture all finished for the day?' Adam said coldly.

She shook her head slowly, standing up to his flashing dark eyes. If he gave her instant notice now, she didn't care. She intended saying all that she felt at that moment.

'You're doing exactly as you say your father did. Switching off the emotions when it doesn't suit you to look into your own heart, Adam. In you, it works differently, because you're mature enough to freeze anybody at will. Poor Susan has only her temper to resort to. I'm sorry for both of you.'

In the silence that almost crackled with tension, Adam gave a sudden grating laugh.

'I was cleverer than I thought when I hired you, Miss Roberts! Chaperone and character-analyst all rolled up into one. Did you ever think of taking up social work on the side?' he said mockingly.

Brie flushed. 'You can sneer all you like,' she said quietly. 'But think about it sometime when you're not being the big-shot tycoon, will you? Sometimes other people can see things more clearly than you can, even when they're right under your nose.'

She moved away from him towards the villa. Her legs were trembling. Her last words had an extra poignant meaning for her. She thanked her stars that he couldn't see what was staring him right in the face. That Brie Roberts loved him, hopelessly loved him, and it was tearing her apart to see him so unable to cope with Susan when with a little more tact and a lot more time, between them they might have made everything right. As it was, Brie guessed that Susan was possibly heading for a breakdown if she didn't loosen up somehow.

'Brie.' She heard him call her name. She turned. He still sat on the garden chair, his head twisted towards her.

'We leave around three o'clock this afternoon. Tell Juanita we'll have a light lunch in half an hour, please.'

He turned away from her, and Brie felt the frustration Susan must feel, of just not getting through to him. Or else of getting through so effectively that Adam had switched her off. Was that the way it had happened at the beach? she wondered now, with sudden insight. Did he know how she felt? But then, wasn't he the kind of man to cash in on such a situation? Unless...unless it had meant something to him too. And that was something so impossibly unlikely she wouldn't even consider it. Instead, she went to inform Juanita of their movements, and to go in search of Susan.

She was in her room, face up on the bed, staring at the ceiling, her face darkly flushed. Pottsy lay across her feet, growling slightly at Brie's approach.

'Susan, I'm sorry you can't come to London,' she said gently. 'But we'll be back tomorrow night, and in a few days I'm sure you'll meet Claire. You'll like her. She knows so much about books—'

'It doesn't matter about London,' Susan's voice was distant. 'I knew he wouldn't let me, anyway. He never does. He only sends me there for school so he can be rid of me.'

'That's just not true and you know it. You have to go to school!'

'Why not here, then? Or in Athens, so I could get home more often. I know a girl who's going to a marvellous school in Athens in September. Why can't I go there, as well? Adam could easily fix it. He's such a pig.'

Brie swallowed the urge to laugh, since Susan was so serious.

'I wish you'd stop calling him that silly word, and come on downstairs. Or help me pack this tea-set, will you? We have to leave about three o'clock, and I haven't put all the tissue paper around the pieces yet. Come on, or I'll be miserable all the way to London, and I can't be miserable when I'm going to a wedding! Friend?'

At last Susan gave her the ghost of a smile and reluctantly got off the bed. She spoke grudgingly.

'Is she really nice, this Claire?'

'She's really nice,' Brie said.

'Nice as you?'

Brie laughed, her eyes dancing as she gave Susan a little push out of the room. 'I'm not answering that, since I'm not at all sure what reply I shall get! I'm not being caught out by that one. I'll just let you decide for yourself when you meet her.'

At least they were communicating again, Brie thought with relief. And Susan handled the pieces of glazed pottery with great care, placing them reverently into the box once they were wrapped in tissue paper. It was far easier on the nerves to be friendly with Susan than anything else. She was tempted to suggest that Susan should be polite towards Adam over lunch, but there was no need. They simply avoided speaking to each other whenever possible, and when they did it was with the utmost civility. Brie could have knocked both their heads together.

She was glad when they left for the small airport where half a dozen private planes were housed. Adam drove them there, then led her towards his small Cessna. Brie felt more nervous than she expected. It was one thing to fly in a commercial aircraft, but she had never been in anything seemingly so small, or so flimsy!

'Don't worry. You'll love it when you get used to it,' Adam commented, seeing her look.

'Are you going to guarantee that?' she asked. She climbed inside, feeling that she was taking her life in her hands. She trusted Adam's expertise, but she couldn't trust her heart not to quake a little. She strapped herself in with shaking hands, and he reached over and fastened the buckle securely. His face came close to hers.

'Do you think I'd let anything happen to you?' he said abruptly. 'You'll be in London before you know it, Brie.'

He started the engine, and the roar was deafening in such a confined space. Brie didn't attempt to talk until they were safely airborne, and although she admitted it was an exhilarating feeling, she was still nervous enough to cover it by speaking too fast.

'Adam, why don't you let Susan go to some school in Athens she's been hearing about? Would it be so lowering to your pride to let her have her own way in this? Maybe she could get home for weekends from Athens. Is that possible? It's what she wants, and I think it's what she needs. You haven't asked for my opinion, but I'm giving it to you anyway.'

'And short of jettisoning you from the plane, I have no choice but to sit and listen to you, right?' Adam said drily.

'Won't you even think about it?'

The plane lurched and dipped, sending Brie's heart somewhere midway between her throat and her feet. She wouldn't admit how scared she felt. She just clung to the seat and hoped he wouldn't notice the whiteness of her knuckles!

'I'll think about it,' he said finally, while she was still praying she wouldn't lose her dignity and throw up.

It was a beginning, she thought. He'd think about it. She glanced at his handsome face, the profile sharply defined against the blue sky outside. A Greek god in every way, she thought again.

'Adam, I really don't mean to interfere in your life,' she said awkwardly. 'It's just that I'm genuinely concerned about Susan.'

She felt the sudden warmth of his hand closing over hers for a moment before he returned his own to the controls.

'I know it.' He sounded as though he believed her. 'And odd as it may seem, I'm quite liking a little interference in my life. I won't always agree with it, but it's nice to know somebody cares.'

She couldn't look at him. If she did and he looked at her, he must surely see just how much she cared. And he was merely indulging her. Out of a sense of guilt towards Susan, perhaps, but at least she had made him think of Susan as a person at last, and not just as a nuisance, an unfortunate legacy...

# CHAPTER 9

In the time that Brie had been away, Claire had changed. She wasn't beautiful, but she glowed with the radiance that only love could bring. When Adam delivered Brie safely to her old home, she and Claire fell on each other's necks, while Bill grinned delightedly in the background. His life, too, had changed direction since meeting Adam Andrikos.

'You look wonderful, Brie,' Claire gasped. 'But then, you always do. Something out there must suit you very well!'

'Call it the climate,' Brie smiled, still a bit shaky after the flight, and glad to get her feet on land again. 'There's no need to ask how you are—nor Bill! It positively shines out of you both.'

'While you all renew old acquaintance, I'll be getting back to my flat,' Adam put in. 'I'll pick you up in the morning, Bill, and you two girls be ready when the taxi arrives for you, serene and beautiful, all right?'

Until that moment, Brie had almost forgotten he had a life of his own in London. He would have people to see, things to do. She was suddenly grateful to him for sparing the time to go out to Corfu especially to bring her here. He didn't have to do that. She wanted to tell him so, but the moment was lost as he became businesslike and told Claire with rough affection not to go getting all maudlin or he'd reverse his offer of the apartment in Corfu. Then he was gone, and it was odd to look around the room she had shared with Claire and see the wedding gifts stacked on the table, and evidence of Bill's belongings strewn about, and the suitcases ready packed for tomorrow. Already, the two of them were a complete unit, and she was the interloper. It was even odder to feel that way, and she was almost embarrassedly conscious of Bill's proprietary presence in what had so recently been Brie's domain.

But he didn't linger, saying with a laugh that he knew the girls would have plenty to talk about, and he still had to settle a few details before tomorrow. Brie went discreetly into the tiny kitchenette while they said their good-byes. It was only then that she recalled the brief exchange of words between Adam and Bill, while Claire was exclaiming on how wonderful she looked...

'You got together with Helen on the script, Bill? She's a miracle worker, I promise you.'

'You needn't tell me! I couldn't believe my eyes when I saw how much work she'd done on it already.'

'And you're happy with the result? Helen's a good buddy. She won't mess you around too much, but I know that some of your dialogue was too tricky to be said aloud, so it had to be simplified in places. Actors don't like tongue-twisters.'

'That's O.K,' Bill said readily, obviously the easiest of writers to work with. 'Just as long as the storyline isn't changed drastically and the central characters stay true to the way I wrote them, I've no objection.'

And the only phrases that stuck in Brie's mind were that Helen was a *miracle worker* and a *good buddy*. She wouldn't have applied either of those to the lady, but clearly Adam saw Helen in quite a different way, and he'd known her longer. Brie pushed the thoughts away as she and

Claire were finally alone, and smiled at her friend.

'No need to ask if you're happy,' she said with a hint of huskiness in her voice. 'It's like watching the sun come up!'

'Good Lord, is it?' Claire laughed. 'And what about you? Are you happy, Brie? Anything to report yet?'

'Why do people in your state always want to see everyone else married off?' Brie fenced. 'Is it some masochistic need to want everyone else hog-tied as well?'

'Come on, love, that's not like you!' Claire knew her too well. 'I really thought that you and Adam—'

'Well, stop thinking it!' Brie said, keeping her voice light. 'We both enjoy the fancy-free life, and that's the way it's going to stay, so forget all about match-making, all right?'

She squeezed Claire's arm, breezing back to the kitchenette to make coffee, saying she might as well do a few final chores in the place, but mostly to escape her friend's sudden puzzled frown. She didn't want to cast any blight on Claire right now, and she didn't want to talk about herself and Adam. She didn't want to think of might-have-beens.

Next day, it was hardly possible to avoid such thoughts. The taxi arrived on time, and Claire was a radiant bride. Brie got a lump in her throat just looking at her. The two of them caused a small stir as they arrived at the register office, and Brie felt a shock at the crowd there at this supposedly quiet wedding.

'The news must have leaked out after all,' Claire exclaimed. 'Oh, Brie—' she sounded suddenly nervous, and Brie held her hand tightly, though her own nerves were starting to jump. There were press cameras in evidence, and she could only guess what the tabloids would make of their appearance outside here after the wedding. Claire and Bill...and Adam Andrikos and his angel of the evening. None of them would have forgotten that already...

'Keep calm and keep smiling,' she told Claire firmly. 'You're the star attraction today, so act like a star! Bill's depending on you, darling, so don't let him down.'

Claire took a deep breath and stepped out of the taxi to gasps of pleasure from the crowd. She looked truly lovely, Brie thought, and knew that her own appearance was attracting attention too. The brief ordeal outside was soon over, and inside the coolness of the register office, the two dark-suited figures awaited them, Bill and Adam. There was no need for Bill to tell Claire how beautiful she looked. To him, she would always be beautiful. And there was no need for words between Adam and herself, Brie thought, but he said the words all the same.

'You look simply sensational,' he murmured in her ear when he had dutifully admired Claire's appearance and the other couple had preceded them into the small chapel-like room where the ceremony was to be performed. 'This should be you and me, don't you think? We look the part!'

Brie's heart lurched painfully at the thoughtless remark. He could have no idea how poignant it was to her, she thought tremulously as he tucked her hand in his arm now. She had to answer him flippantly, or she'd probably have said something terribly sentimental and humiliate herself.

'Don't let the appearance fool you, Adam. I'm only the supporting role. I'll be back to my nursemaid duties tomorrow, which is what I'm being paid to do. But thanks for this little bonus all the same.'

Employer and employee, that's all they

were, she reminded herself, and it didn't do to forget it.

She forgot everything in the next ten minutes as the simple ceremony began. The reverence was the same as if it was a large church wedding, the vows and responses, and the love between the couple making their replies in low, intense voices. From this day forward, for better or worse, Claire and Bill belonged together...Brie's throat was thick, her hands slightly damp as she clutched the bouquet of red roses Claire had handed her while she became Bill's wife. The scent of them drifted into her nostrils. Red roses for love. They were so heady that she felt as if she were almost drowning in their scent. If the press cameras outside had been an ordeal, then this was so much more, with the man Brie loved standing motionless by her side, unaware of how turbulent were her emotions.

And then it was over and Bill kissed his bride. Everyone hugged everyone else, and Brie hardly knew how she came to be held in Adam's arms with his mouth on hers, and the wedding bouquet in danger of being crushed between them until Claire laughingly managed to extricate it. Adam's kiss was unimaginably sweet, dangerously familiar, and she felt intoxicated by the man and the scent of the roses...she pulled away from him when she decided the kiss had gone on just too long.

The fact that she could have blissfully have stayed in his arms all day and that Claire at least was perfectly aware of it, sent the warm colour to her cheeks. She was thankful when they had done with the formalities and on their way out into the sunshine. Only to gasp at the sudden deafening click of cameras and the surge forward of the crowd that seemed to have grown to ridiculous proportions now.

The photographer Bill had hired was hard pressed to keep the rest of them back to take his official ones.

'Keep smiling. It'll all be over soon,' Adam murmured in Claire's ear.

Would it? Brie wondered. She had heard the word 'angel' among the crowd, and groaned inwardly, guessing what the press would make of this. Adam had several British newspapers sent to Corfu daily, so they would soon know.

'Right, that's enough,' Adam said, once the official photographs were done. 'Follow me, all of you.'

To Brie's surprise, he turned and went back inside the building again, leading them all through a side door where the taxi was waiting for them. He had expected all this, Brie thought suspiciously. Maybe he'd even engineered it. In his job, any publicity was good for the ratings, she supposed, even to cashing in on a friend's wedding.

Was that why she'd been invited along? To add to the speculation about Adam and herself? To keep the story alive, and including the romance of his angel's best friend and his new writer for the TV series? Brie felt so enraged she couldn't think straight. It all fitted, but there was no way she could tackle him about it—yet. Not while Claire and Bill were laughing so ecstatically at the way they had fooled the press and got away to the safety of Adam's club, where the room given to the small wedding party was exclusively for the four of them. Not yet...

By mid-afternoon they had returned to Claire's home to change out of their finery, and the men had gone to collect Bill's cases. There was hardly time to think then, before Adam had whisked them all away, the taxi loaded with suitcases, a trusted neighbour in the building promising to keep an eye on the wedding presents while Claire was away until she and Bill sorted out their long-term future plans later. The series was being rushed to get it out in the late autumn if possible and life promised to be hectic from now on. Brie had had no idea how fast the TV people could work once they had a deadline. Teamwork was incredible, providing you had a good team and a good leader. She thought of Adam, and couldn't deny that he'd be that all right. Remembering the crisp dynamic talk he'd given at the sci-fi convention, it wasn't hard to guess that he'd bring out the best in his team. It was only Brie in which he brought out the worst...Brie, and his sister Susan, she added.

They reached Corfu by late evening, and Brie felt exhausted by then. The mental strain of the day and the nervousness she felt in the light aircraft were beginning to tell. She asked Adam to drop her at the villa while he drove Claire and Bill to their honeymoon apartment. Claire hugged her at the last moment and said she'd be seeing her soon.

'But not too soon,' Bill teased. 'We'll give you a call.'

'Be happy, both of you,' Brie said huskily, and couldn't say any more. She ran into the villa, right into Susan's belligerent face.

'I thought you'd be back earlier,' she said accusingly. 'I've been waiting for you all afternoon. Where's Adam? Didn't he come in with you? He hasn't gone off already, has he?'

Brie's temper exploded.

'No, you irritating child, he hasn't gone off already. He's just taken Claire and Bill to the apartment, and of course we couldn't have got back sooner. Have you any idea how long it takes for a private plane to get to Corfu? We did have a wedding to go to, you know,' she finished sarcastically, 'and the bride and groom do deserve some consideration, like having their photos taken, and being given a proper send-off, with food and champagne, or had that escaped your tiny, selfish narrow little mind?'

She stopped, appalled, at the shocked look on Susan's face. She'd never spoken to her quite so furiously before, and it didn't help when she caught sight of Helen

Churchill coming out of the sitting-room, a glass of wine in her hand, an interested look on her face, obviously having heard the whole thing.

'Poor you,' Helen said, falsely sympathetic. 'It must have been a terrible day with all that gadding about. I can see you're not used to it, darling, and Susan shouldn't have burst out at you like that. Why don't you go and lie down and take an aspirin or something? Susan and I will wait for Adam to get home, and I'll tell him you're just exhausted, Brie.'

The tone was so sweet it was unbelievable. The words put Brie neatly into the ancient nanny mould, unused to fast living and the frenetic world of which Helen and Adam were both a part. If it hadn't been so damnably true that she was near to dropping, Brie would have turned on her too. But that would have been just what Helen expected, she thought keenly, and she had no desire to act so undignified with the other girl. Neither did she really want to see Adam again that night. When she did, she wanted her head clear and to demand to know his motives for today's trip to England.

'You do that,' she said coolly to Helen.

'We've seen enough of one another since we left here yesterday. I've hardly had a moment to myself, and it'll be good to take a shower and go to bed to sleep.'

And she could make what she liked of that, Brie thought! She left Helen still staring after her with a stab of anger in her eyes, while Susan was grumbling as usual and not realising the verbal warfare she had just witnessed.

Brie wilted when she reached her own room. Her small case was still in Adam's car, but it didn't matter. Tomorrow would do. The thought of sleep was more appealing than anything else, but first she forced herself to take a quick warm shower to relax her tension then, slipping a thin nightdress over her head, she almost crawled into bed, snapping out the light at once.

She had expected to lie awake, despite her tiredness, her nerves too taut with remembering the day. Claire and Bill together now in some magical world of their own...Adam...but she fell asleep immediately, as if to block out all the fantasies, all the impossible dreams...

She awoke on the instant her door clicked

open, swivelling her head and feeling it spin from moving it too fast. There was a dark shape outlined in the doorway, faintly lit from the soft landing light. Brie felt her heart begin to pound as the shape moved inside the door and closed it behind him.

'What do you want?' she croaked. Her voice seemed dried up in her throat. She couldn't see him properly. Her hand stretched out to put on her bedside lamp and hesitated. Did she really want him to see her half-asleep, her hair tousled on the pillow, her eyes still half-open? Did she want to be here in the darkness with him...? She switched on the light.

Adam was still in the clothes he'd worn on the plane. In his hand he held her suitcase. His eyes were frankly amused as she realised she was clutching the sheet up to her chin like some frightened schoolgirl. She released it a fraction.

'I live here,' he commented drily. 'And I did knock. I thought you might be in need of this case. I hardly expected you to be asleep already. I've just been giving the others a quick run-down on the day's events—'

'You mean they were actually interested?' she said before she stopped to think, heavy with sarcasm. She didn't think Helen would be interested in anyone's wedding but her own—and was quite convinced now that she had her sights firmly set on Adam Andrikos to fill the bridegroom's role.

Adam's eyes glinted. 'What's wrong with you? I know you too well, Brie. Something's been bugging you for hours, hasn't it? You covered it up pretty well from Claire and Bill, but I'm not moving from this room until you tell me.'

He sat down heavily on the bed, arms folded. The nerve of him, Brie thought furiously. Acting like some kind of Dutch uncle now, with herself cast in the kind of role Susan was best suited for and was never allowed to fulfil. And she didn't want this kind of wise understanding from him right now, damn it. She didn't want his placid smoothing over of her apparent female capriciousness. Her feelings erupted. She sat straight up in bed, her eyes blazing at him.

'You want to know what's wrong? I'll tell you what's wrong, Adam! I feel as if I've been used as part of some publicity stunt, that's what! I suspect that you wanted me to go to London with you to further that stupid newspaper story about your elusive angel! I think it was you who tipped off the press to be at the register office, and it wouldn't surprise me in the least if you hadn't teased them with the thought that it might be *you* getting married—'

As she paused for breath, he broke in angrily.

'With you as my temperamental bride, I suppose? Perish the thought!'

'My feelings exactly,' Brie said in a choked voice.

He suddenly leaned forward and seized her by the shoulders, glowering into her eyes. The entire episode had happened so fast it had shaken her nerves even more, and she was hardly aware of how her nipples had hardened against the cool fabric of her nightdress, or how the sheet had fallen to her waist, or how her mouth was trembling. She hardly noticed the shimmer of tears on her lashes, brought about by sheer fatigue and frustration and the shock of this encounter with Adam.

But he noticed all those things, and his initial intention of shaking some sense into her changed instead to a rigid grip on her upper arms.

'Am I really so obnoxious to you?' he demanded. 'Do you hate me that much?'

'Yes!' Brie almost sobbed. 'Yes, yes, yes...oh...no! I don't hate you, Adam...I just don't understand you, that's all. We're poles apart, and I'd much prefer it if we stuck to our business arrangement, that's all! I'm trying to do my best for Susan...'

He swore softly, looking intently into her eyes.

'We're not discussing Susan for the moment. But I'm damned if I care for that look of sheer terror I saw when I came into your room. What did you think I was going to do to you? Do you think me capable of hurting you?'

Brie swallowed weakly. 'You *are* hurting me,' she said, her voice thick with holding back the tears. 'You're hurting my arms. And I wasn't afraid, just startled—'

He let go of his powerful hold on her and looked at the reddened marks from his fingers. Before she could think what he intended, he had pulled her close and gently kissed each bare shoulder, his lips cool and caressing. The movement was so tender and so unexpected, Brie knew those tears were getting ever nearer to the surface, and she couldn't bear to let him know it.

'I'm sorry,' Adam said softly. 'About a lot of things. And I want you to know I hadn't planned any of today's press coverage. I want you to believe that, Brie. It's important to me that you do. Sure, I arranged for the taxi to be at the other door, once I saw the cameras out front, but my guess is that it was Bill's photographer who tipped them off. Why not? It will do his business some good to have newspaper celebrities in his shop window enlargements. We all have to make a living, darling.'

It made sense, she supposed. And she wanted to believe that was the way it happened. She wanted to believe him. His eyes were very close to hers, studying them. She could see the honesty there, and knew instinctively that doing anything so underhand wasn't Adam's styie. If he wanted newspaper coverage, he was flamboyant enough to go ahead and get it without resorting to trickery.

'I'm sorry too,' she mumbled. 'I can't seem to think straight about anything—and Adam, I am worried about Susan, you know. Really worried.' She had to bring Susan's name into this, because suddenly the situation was too supercharged with emotion. And because she couldn't bear it for Adam to go on looking at her that way, when she yearned to put her arms around him and beg him to stay. The feeling was so strong it scared her. She dug her hands into the bed as if to prevent herself from doing so, and he felt the tensing of her muscles beneath his fingers. He leaned forward and touched her lips with his own. It wasn't a kiss of passion, but his mouth lingered on hers, excitingly gentle, as if he was reluctant to break away from the contact. He spoke softly against her mouth, and the sensation was unbearably erotic to her heightened senses.

'Stop worrying, Brie. I've given your suggestion some thought.'

She pulled away from him then. This was too vital not to pursue it properly.

'To let her go to school in Athens, you mean? In September?'

He laughed shortly. His hands still ran a leisurely trail up and down her bare arms, making her shiver. She put one hand over his, stilling the movement, capturing his fingers. He interlocked them with hers, his thumb gently moving against her skin.

'Are you so confident I can fix it, as Susan would say? At such short notice?

The school she has in mind is exclusive and expensive and places are scarce—'

'If anyone can fix it, you can,' Brie said to her own surprise. 'I have no doubt about that, so will you try, Adam, please? For—for Susan's own sake?'

'And for yours, because I've never met such an irritatingly persistent, caring, wonderful nursemaid before,' he retorted. 'As it happens, I know one of the governors of the school very well. I see no problem—but until it's definite, I'd rather you said nothing to Susan about this. It's to be our secret for the time being, or we forget it. Do you agree? I don't want her crowing over me every minute she's on vacation!'

'Agreed,' Brie said quickly. She could hardly believe it. Nor that she and Adam were now some kind of conspirators. She felt so delighted she could hardly speak, and her mouth broke into a huge smile as she held out her hand to shake his in agreement. Adam merely laughed, ignoring it, and this time he didn't stop at a gentle kiss. He caught her to his body, crushing her against him so that her arms reached out to hold him as she was caught off-balance. Her hair fell away from her shoulders as she was arched into his embrace, and the pressure on her mouth deepened and lengthened, and then she was eased back onto the bed with his mouth still possessing hers, his body half covering hers. She wasn't aware when she was no longer struggling to resist him, but was responding as passionately to his kiss, to the caresses of his hands on her body, to the needs she felt in him. This was her love, her destiny, and this the only ending to an emotion-filled day...

He moved away from her abruptly, and she could hear him breathing more heavily than ususal. He touched one finger to the passion-soft lips he had just kissed.

'Call that my payment,' he said lightly, and then she felt the pressure of his body removed from her bed. In a few easy strides he was across the room and gone, and Brie lay there motionless, unsure whether to be relieved or utterly frustrated. Either way, she was furious at his words, as if she had bargained for this...but she was too spent to use up any more energy on fury. She couldn't think any more. She buried her head in the pillow and let herself drift into imaginary black velvet.

Since it was Sunday the next day, everyone slept late, and it was only the sense that someone was bouncing on her bed that roused Brie irritably. Susan was dressed in shorts and tee shirt, and demanding to know if she was coming for a swim.

'When I'm properly awake and I've had some coffee,' Brie groaned. 'Get Adam to go with you or something—'

'Adam's gone to the hotel where his people are staying,' Susan announced with a scowl. 'He says they still have to work even though it's Sunday, to keep on schedule. I bet your honeymooners aren't working today!'

Brie threw off the bedclothes. 'I should think not! You get out of here and give me fifteen minutes, and I'll be right down. Toast and coffee at the double, all right?'

'Are you giving me orders now?' Susan asked imperiously.

Brie gave her bottom a playful smack. 'That's right. Now scoot. Lemon marmalade, please,' she added as she made for her bathroom.

It evidently worked, because by the time she was washed and dressed, Susan was in the kitchen and pouring out two mugs of coffee. A pile of toast was waiting on a tray, with two plates and knives and a pot of lemon marmalade.

'You're improving,' Brie smiled at the girl. 'Shall we take it out on the patio in the sun?'

Susan agreed. She may not say so, but she was clearly glad to see Brie and Adam back again. And when she went to school in Athens? Adam would still be in England most of the time, Brie supposed, but at least Susan would be within easy access of home, and that would mean a lot to her. She dearly wished she could have told her right now, but she remembered her agreement with Adam, and said nothing. She just prayed it would go through as easily as Adam had predicted. At the first opportunity Brie intended reminding him to get on to it right away.

The chance didn't come until that evening. She had seen nothing of Adam until then, and she and Susan had spent a reasonably pleasant day, swimming at the beach and watching an old movie on television when the sun got too hot for them to stay outside.

Adam didn't come home until shortly before dinner, and then he was bad-tempered and pre-occupied, and it was pretty obvious that the day hadn't gone well, to put it mildly.

'Lord preserve me from temperamental actors,' he snapped, when Susan asked him recklessly what had got under his skin today.

Brie kept a poker face. He wasn't exactly untemperamental himself, although he'd never admit to it, of course. She had avoided thinking too much about last night, knowing she would be too embarrassed to face him if she dwelt on it too deeply. But one look at his darkly tense face, and she knew she needn't have worried. He was too wrapped up in his work to remember the scene in her room. But he had to remember about Susan, Brie thought fiercely. Brie might be unimportant to him, but Susan's whole future was at stake here. If the girl wasn't to become totally neurotic before she was out of her teens, Adam must see that letting her come home, in effect, by means of this school in Athens, was helping her take an enormous step back to normality after her parents' deaths.

When Susan said she was going to take Pottsy for a walk after dinner, Brie took her courage in both hands and followed Adam along to his study. They'd been capable of holding an intelligent conversation there before, so she hoped that was a good omen. The moment she saw his face as he snapped into the phone, she knew it wasn't. He waved her to sit down, and she sat, feeling as though she was facing some irascible headmaster.

'You'll have to speak to Helen about it, Mark. Hades is on his honeymoon, for pity's sake, and I'm not disturbing him until tomorrow at the earliest! Sort it out with Helen. That's what she's being paid for.' He slammed down the receiver, running his fingers through his black hair in a fury. He expected perfection from everyone around him, because he himself was a perfectionist, but he didn't always get it. Brie's brief sympathy ran out as he glared at her, his mind still elsewhere.

'What is it, Brie?' he asked tightly. 'I've a million things to do here—'

'I'm sorry. This isn't a good time, I know, but if you'd just remember to contact the school in Athens about Susan, Adam. I just wanted to remind you. Put a note on your desk or—or something, to call them tomorrow—' She floundered, seeing the incredulous look on his face.

'Good God, woman, I can't be thinking of that right now! I've a series to shoot and the whole thing's in utter chaos at the moment. The actors are disagreeing with each other and fighting over camera space, and the costume designers aren't coming up with the right materials to make the *Demons of Darkness* look authentic, and you come bothering me with domestic details like this—'

'They aren't *details!* Adam, last night, you promised—'

'Last night I didn't have this lot to worry about,' he threw back at her. 'I'll fix it. I told you. But not now. Leave it with me, and it'll be done. O.K? Now just leave me alone, will you? I have to get through to London.' His hand was already reaching for the phone again, his voice clipped and urgent. He wasn't really seeing her or listening to her, Brie thought incredulously. No wonder Susan was the way she was. No wonder she felt so unloved, so much a responsibility and no more. She knew exactly how the girl must feel. She turned on her heel and stalked out of Adam's study, only just resisting the urge to throw something at him first and slam the door second.

# CHAPTER 10

There was a note of apology pushed under Brie's door the next morning.

'It's not always like this,' Adam wrote in his large firm handwriting. 'Only at the beginning when tempers get frayed, and it seems as though we've taken on something impossible. It'll all start to get unravelled soon, I promise you. And I've written myself a note reminding me to phone A. Forgiven?'

Brie presumed that the A referred to Athens. She wondered if he thought Susan wasn't averse to peeking at a note in Brie's room, and found herself agreeing that he was probably right.

It wasn't much of an apology, but it was something, she conceded. And it proved that he'd thought about her words after all. At least about letting Susan change schools. He made no reference, ever, to the lack of communication between himself and Susan over their parents' deaths. It was a subject that seemed taboo to them both. Adam was able to immerse himself in work, and was adult enough to face grief squarely, while Susan...

It worried Brie to see how brittle the girl was at times. As if she was made of glass that was all ready to splinter, and when she did...

The two of them were having breakfast when the phone rang, prior to Susan's morning stint of lessons with Miss Vesey. Juanita took the call and told Brie it was for her. An English lady.

'Claire? How wonderful! I didn't expect to hear from you for days yet,' Brie said teasingly. 'Not tired of married life already, are you?'

'No way!' Claire was bright and bubbly, even at this early hour. 'Only Bill got the royal command last night, to report to the hotel this morning, since there was some kind of uproar about the script. He didn't really want to get involved, but Adam said he was entitled to have the last word on it, as it was his book. Bill suspected that this was Adam's way of settling things without getting personally involved, but since Adam's been so kind and generous to us, he could hardly refuse. Anyway, we knew he'd be working here, and we'll be together every night, so I think I can spare him during the day! So can we get together, Brie? We haven't had a good old heart to heart for ages, have we?'

'Come over to the villa this morning,' Brie said at once. 'Susan has her lessons, and we can go down to the beach before it gets too hot. I'm sure Miguel will drive over and fetch you and take you back later.'

'Wonderful. I'll be ready any time.' She hung up.

It would be great, Brie told herself. But she guessed that Claire sensed there was something wrong, and was dying to find out what it was. And Brie had been so determined not to tell her. By the time the two of them were happily at the beach, stretched out in swimsuits on the warm sand, Brie had already decided to make Susan's problems the topic of conversation rather than her own.

'And the poor kid never cries about *anything?*' Claire echoed. 'It's not natural. When I was her age, the slightest thing would set me off. It's all part of that painful growing-up process, isn't it? You should know all about it, Brie, with your training.'

'I do know, and you're right. She's really hung-up about her parents, I'm convinced of it, but because of some misguided comment by her father, she can't express it. And Adam's hardly the one to help her. He's never around when she needs him, and when they meet they're at each others' throats half the time.'

'And you're caught in the middle of it,' Claire finished for her. 'I don't envy you, Brie. I mean, Adam's gorgeous, but I'd say he's got a temper when he's roused, hasn't he?'

'Just a bit,' Brie grinned at the understatement.

'Then he's a match for you,' Claire said lazily, lying back on the sand and closing her eyes blissfully as the sun caressed her skin. 'I aways knew you two were meant for each other.'

'You wouldn't say that if you knew how many times we've clashed,' Brie said.

'Oh well, the making up is always better when you've had a real belter of a fight,' Claire wouldn't be swayed. 'Remember, I saw the way he looked at you when you first met, and I saw the way you looked at each other at my wedding. You can't fool me, Brie!'

It was pointless to try. It was better simply to say nothing, Brie decided. She changed the conversation neatly.

'How does Bill feel about the script-writer taking over his book? Is it causing him any problems?'

'I don't think so.' Claire shook her head. 'He's relieved in a way, because he doesn't know the first thing about adapting novels for TV, and working with Helen Churchill for the past ten days in London, it's given him enormous insight into what's right and what's wrong as far as a different medium is concerned. He's full of admiration for her, Brie. She's worked non-stop on the script since it got into her hands, and she's acknowledged to be the best. Aren't we lucky?'

Brie nodded, her feelings very different from Claire's! But she couldn't begrudge Bill his luck in getting the best script-writer to do justice to his book.

Claire stayed for lunch at the villa, and a quick call to the TV people's hotel to leave a message for Bill to pick her up around five o'clock when he'd finished for the day meant she could stay all afternoon. By the end of it, she told Brie caustically that she didn't envy her Susan's company.

The girl had joined them at the beach and was as prickly as gorse. When she tired of the two English girls, she flounced off back to the villa, saying she was taking Pottsy back for his lunch, and Claire breathed a sigh of relief.

'You know what? I think she was jealous of our friendship, Brie. She wanted you all to herself!'

'You could be right, but I'm not fooling myself that she's getting fond of me. The only thing she gives affection to is that dog—and Adam, when he allows it! I'm more of a sounding-board most of the time.'

'Well, we all need that, don't we?' Claire commented.

When they got back to the villa, the English newspapers had arrived. Adam always had them sent out on the first available flight each day, so that he was up to the minute in current affairs. And there on the front page of two of them were four smiling faces. At first glance it could be taken for a double wedding, and Brie wished immediately that she hadn't bought the frivolous hat with the flattering veiling. Especially when she read the caption beneath.

'Adam Andrikos and his angel attend wedding of best-selling author Diablo Hades and his bride, Claire. Will Adam and the angel be next? It's odds on that they will, say close friends.'

'What close friends?' Brie said, enraged. 'It wasn't anything to do with you, was it, Claire?'

'Of course not.' She looked honestly shocked. 'It's just newspaper jargon. You should know all about that by now! Don't let it bother you, Brie.'

'I won't,' she said grimly. 'But it just might bother some other people.'

Namely Adam and Susan and Helen Churchill, to name a formidable trio. She flipped through the other newspapers. The arch captions were all similar, and Brie fumed at being thrust into the limelight once more. If it was deserved, she'd have probably been ecstatic. As it was, it was painful to read.

Bill picked up Claire and they went off with one of the papers, delighted and thrilled to have made the front page. Adam was slower to comment as he went through the papers that were left.

'We make a good-looking couple, don't we?' He asked without false modesty.

'Nearly as good as the bride and groom.'

He was being generous. His own physique and flamboyance, and Brie's delicate English beauty far outshone that of the other couple, except for the new-mint look of happiness in Claire's and Bill's eyes.

'They got it all wrong again,' she retorted flippantly. 'Is this all part of the game too? Nobody wins but the newspaper bosses when the circulation goes up, right? Gossip taking precedence over matters of world importance like summit talks, or local tragedies like poor old ladies being mugged for their pension money—'

'Don't let it get to you, Brie,' Adam said calmly, as her voice lost its lightness and became impassioned.

'No? How long before one of their bright young reporters decides to come out here and start taking pictures and wanting interviews? I either end up appearing as a kept woman, or a liar, or just jilted when they see it's all such a stupid mistake. I don't like the image. How much damage do you think all this is doing to my career? I care for other people's children. I'm responsible for their health and their morals while I'm in charge of them. When

I leave here, I'll expect a reference from you, as usual. If you make it terse, it will be bad enough. If it's too glowing, any future employer will draw his own conclusion after reading this newspaper garbage—'

'Don't you think you're over-reacting to all this?' Adam said coldly. 'I deal with this sort of publicity every day, and it hasn't ruined by career—'

'But you don't work with children! It's totally different!' She almost shouted in frustration. The truth of what she was saying had only just struck her, and now she wondered just how far-reaching the effects of all this unwelcome publicity was going to be. She liked her work. She had always had a great empathy with children, particularly the very young, and she couldn't bear to have her good name jeopardised in any way.

'Maybe I'd better make an honest woman of you then. Is that the answer?' Adam said coolly. 'Give the tabloids what they're waiting for and then we can retire gracefully into obscurity. You can even start a brood of your own kids, yours and mine. From personal experience, I can vouch for the fact that you won't damage their tiny minds by any kind of loose morality.'

He watched her intently as he spoke, and the hot colour flooded her cheeks. He degraded marriage and parenthood by his brashness. She almost choked on her reply.

'You can be very hateful when you choose to be—'

'I know. I find it's often the best way of getting an honest reaction,' his voice was clipped. 'Well, since you've so charmingly declined my proposal, we'd better decide what to do about the newshounds. I doubt very much if they'll come out here, but if it worries you I can always cable a retraction, insist that there's no question of marriage between us. I can invent a fiancé for you, if you like—or find one of my own. One fantasy will always cancel out another—'

'No.' She couldn't think straight. Did he seriously think he'd made her a marriage proposal? It would just serve him right if she'd taken him at his word and accepted! The poignancy of it all made the muscles in her jaws tighten. Her head throbbed. She had had too much sun today, and this confrontation was just about the end.

'Let's just leave it, Adam. It will die a quick death if we ignore it. At least, I can only hope so. At least they didn't print my name this time.'

They just called her his angel...she bit her lip to stop it trembling. She felt his arm around her shoulders and he moved swiftly to her side.

'Brie, I'm sorry about all this. I swear I don't know how it happened and I never thought it would get to you like this. Anyway, nobody in their right minds will see you as a scarlet woman, darling. They only have to look at you and listen to you to know that you're sweet and lovely—' his voice was rougher than before, yet its very roughness was at once protective and tender. Her instinctive response that he made her sound about as sexy as a box of chocolates died on her lips as she realised that he really cared that all this had upset her so much. If his caring went no further, then at least she could be comforted by that.

'You see what I mean?' she mumbled, looking up at him with shimmering eyes. 'You put something like that in my reference, and they'll think—they'll think—'

He bent forward and touched her mouth with his own, a whisper of a kiss. 'Let them think what they like. You have a look of honesty about you, Brie, that instils trust in children. It was one of the reasons I chose you out of all the other applicants for the job. Truth is stranger than fiction, isn't it? If those gossip-mongers want to make more of our relationship than it is, then let them. Just don't let it upset you, that's all.'

At one and the same time he managed to clarify the situation, and remind her that she was here to do a job, and she'd do better to get on with it than turn into some neurotic scatterbrain. It was a pity he couldn't talk so frankly with Susan, she thought bitterly, instead of clamming up every time their emotions began to boil over...she swallowed, seeing the sudden gentleness in his dark eyes.

What she said was right. He could be hateful when he chose to be. He could also be incredibly perceptive and understanding and tender, when he chose to be. How would he react now, if she rushed headlong into suggesting he try talking quietly with Susan, meeting the girl halfway and letting her know he wanted to do his best about arranging the school place in Athens? Did she even dare to broach it right now when

Adam seemed so anxious to calm her?

The decision was taken out of her hands by the arrival of what seemed like a dark tornado into the room. Susan thrust one of the newspapers under both their noses, and to Brie's annoyance, she and Adam both sprang apart instinctively at her presence, as if they had been caught doing something wrong.

'Is anybody going to tell me what's going on around here?' she stormed at them both. 'You didn't get married on the quiet while you were in London, did you? Do I have to start calling Brie sister? I mean, don't mind me! I'm just family, for what it's worth! The whole world will know what's going on before I do, as per usual!'

'Susan, will you shut up!' Adam thundered at her. 'Nothing is going on, as you put it. Brie and I are not married, and have no plans to be, and if we were, we wouldn't consult an idiotic child who thinks she owns the place and everyone in it—'

'I don't think that.' Susan shouted back. 'I don't own anything except Pottsy, do I? I'm nothing to you. You hate me. You always shut me out. Brie doesn't want me now she's got her friend here. They were laughing about things I knew nothing about today. I don't need her any more if she won't talk to me—'

'Susan, that's just not true!' Brie exclaimed at once. She was appalled at the way all the good she thought she'd been achieving with Susan seemed to have been wiped out in a single moment. 'What did you expect me to do when Claire was my guest for the day? Ignore her and spend my time treating you like a baby who needed constant attention every minute? I thought that was exactly what you hated. You're not very consistent, are you?'

'Don't try reasoning with her,' Adam put in angrily. 'What she needs is a good thrashing, and much more of this and she's going to get it. I've had about enough of female tantrums for one day.'

He crossed the room in long strides and slammed the door behind him. Several glass ornaments on a display shelf tinkled alarmingly as the door jamb vibrated. Brie looked at Susan's scarlet face. She took a deep breath.

'I've had about enough too,' she said evenly. 'I've had enough of your nonsense and your bad temper, and I've had enough of trying to be peacemaker between you and Adam. It's not what I'm paid for, and I don't have to put up with it the way he does. I took this job because I care about children and I like to think I have something to offer them. But you don't need anybody, do you? You don't want people to care about you, and you certainly don't need me! The best thing I can do is quit. It's obviously going to suit everyone.'

Susan stared at her. *Why don't you cry?* Brie thought agonisingly. *Why don't you beg?* After the little scene with Adam, and now this ultimatum, any normal child might be bursting into tears right now, but not Susan. She was as tense as a bow string, but she didn't cry. Her hands were clenched tightly at her sides, her face almost convulsed.

'I don't want you to go.' The words were clipped, staccato, brittle.

'Why not?' Brie threw back. 'Do you like having me around as some kind of whipping-boy?'

She felt a grim humour, remembering how Adam had so recently assured her that she instilled trust in children. Not in this one, she didn't. The words tumbled out of Susan in response.

'I don't feel like that about you. It's not like that! You don't understand. Nobody does—' the voice was angry, at herself and the world. Brie's impatience dwindled.

'Why don't you try me then? Make me understand, Susan. I'm your friend, remember?' She held her breath, willing the girl to smile and break up this brittle atmosphere. Instead, she saw the familiar scowl on the other's attractive features, and the dark eyes flashed.

'You've got your own friends,' she said rudely. 'None of my nursemaids has brought them over here before. That proves you're somebody special to Adam, doesn't it?'

She rushed out of the room, Pottsy clamouring at her heels, and as always Brie felt drained. It was clear as daylight that what Susan needed most of all was a proper, normal family life again, and not the thrashing that Adam recommended, however tempting the prospect of that might be! The child was exasperating and tried Brie's patience to the limit, but she could still feel sympathy towards her. She still had the soft heart that went with the stricter demands of the job, and the ability to see everything through a child's eyes.

She ached to help Susan, and had never felt so helpless to know how to act.

She flinched when Adam came back into the room, closing the door quietly this time. What now? Her nerves steeled themselves at once, and then his words took her by surprise.

'I'm sorry about all that,' he was curt, but she sensed that his anger at Susan still smouldered beneath the surface while he made an effort to be calm. 'About the unfortunate publicity our appearance at the wedding has aroused, and about Susan's reaction. But I can only echo Susan's words. I don't want you to go. Despite how it may seem to you, you're the best thing that's happened to her—'

'Were you listening?' Brie said indignantly, hardly hearing anything else.

'Yes,' he said, unabashed. 'And naturally I can't stop you walking out on us, but I'm asking you to stay. For Susan's sake.'

Their gazes clashed, held and locked. Brie felt unable to tear herself away from that burning, intense look he gave her. It seemed to penetrate her thoughts, her senses, her soul, she thought with a rising panic. He knew her indecision, her uncertainty, the need to get away, the longing to stay...she prayed he was unaware of the real reason for her churning emotions. She prayed he couldn't guess how the sudden yearning to rush to him and cup his face in her hands and kiss away all the frustration his sister caused him was almost overwhelming at that moment. The urge was similar to the way she sometimes felt about a hurt child...but that was where the similarity ended, for Brie's feelings towards Adam Andrikos were those of a woman for a man, and she knew that she loved him beyond reason. Otherwise, she'd have said right here and now that she couldn't possibly go on working in such a crazy household. That she would have to leave immediately...

'I'll stay.' She heard her own voice, husky and controlled. 'For—Susan's sake.'

Certainly not for her own, when it was sweet torment to see Adam every day, and know he thought no more of her than a useful member of his staff, and spared the time every now and then to throw her a few crumbs of his male attention. Meaningless, of course, for why should Adam Andrikos, who could have any woman he wanted out of an industry teeming with the most beautiful and elegant, want Brie Roberts, except for a diversion, and because she was here on his doorstep? She allowed herself no illusions, and felt herself tighten in every muscle as Adam moved swiftly towards her. And it was his hands that cupped Brie's cheeks, his face that was suddenly tender with relief as he looked down into her eyes, so close that she could see the lighter flecks in the darkness, she could breathe in the fragrance of his aftershave amid the erratic swiftness of her heartbeats. Again, he touched her mouth with his, and she couldn't pull away without being in danger of having her neck broken by the gentle pressure of his hands. She didn't want to break away...

Without realising, she gave a little sigh of pure pleasure and relaxed the tautness of her stance a fraction to lean her body against Adam's. Without knowing how it happened, her arms had reached out instinctively to steady herself, and now they slid around his back, holding him, and the kiss that had begun so lightly became a sudden flame of desire.

She could feel the hardening of his body as she yielded against it, and the rush of adrenalin in her veins was more potent than any aphrodisiac. If it was crazy, unwise, unethical, for her to submit to her employer's embrace, then so be it. This was no time for thinking, for examining ethics; this was too beautiful a moment, when her spirits were soaring, and an exploding joy was searing through her. Right now there was no right or wrong. There was only this. Brie and Adam, caught in a moment of pure physical need. She wouldn't question anything further.

Here in his arms, as his hands slid down the length of her and moved around her possessively, moving slowly up and down the length of her spine, she could feel the power in the man. Crushed to his chest, her breasts flattened against him, she was aware of his heartbeats, strong, insistent, matching her own so that she was unable to tell them apart.

The slightly roughened chin grazed her soft flesh and only stimulated her need of him more. She felt his fingers tangling in her hair, and her own hands reached upwards to rake through Adam's own, feeling the thick dark virile growth, curling into his nape. She loved every bit of it. She loved the taste of his lips on hers, the gentle foraging of his tongue against hers as her lips parted to his insistent probing. That first touch was like an electric shock rippling over her skin. It was intimate, beyond friendship, crossing new boundaries. She allowed him access to the softness of her inner cheek and felt her senses dance in ecstacy. His thighs were tense against her, one leg moving gently between hers. It was sheer sexuality, and Brie was totally mesmerised by it. What the outcome of it might have been she couldn't guess. The spell was broken by sounds of cars arriving and people talking and footsteps nearing the villa on the gravel outside, and Adam broke away from her reluctantly.

'Stay for my sake too, Brie,' he told her in a low throaty voice, and then he twisted on his heels and went to meet his TV people who had come over from the hotel for a meeting to discuss the day's events, and for dinner.

Brie stood perfectly still for several minutes after he'd gone. Wishing these moments could have lasted for ever. Wishing desperately she didn't have to join these other people that evening, when Adam had made it plain that of course she and Susan were included in any social occasions at the villa. Wishing she needn't look on while the glamorous and the powerful discussed their mutual projects while she felt so inadequate beside them. Wishing it could be just herself and Adam...for always...she let out a long breath, and realised she had been holding it in for a long time until the sunlight on the flowers outside seemed to dance in front of her eyes.

She should have taken her courage in both hands and said that she couldn't stay a minute longer in a place where she wasn't needed. Susan could more than take care of herself...but deep down, Brie knew that just wasn't true. And with those last words, Adam had pushed away any possibility of her walking out.

'Stay for my sake too,' he had said. And the poignancy of it was that he couldn't possibly know how her heart had leapt at those words. He couldn't know how much Brie wished he had meant them in an entirely different context, and not just as a means of smoothing down the ruffled temperament of his unpredictable sister. If only he had meant them...Brie knew she was being the world's worst fool for staying on and torturing herself like this, but stay she would, until Susan was safely installed in the new school in Athens that as yet she knew nothing about. And with that resolve, Brie decided that a strategic note left on Adam's desk in his study to remind him to contact the school might be the best way of going about things. Safer than risking another fight.

Her eyes blurred. They certainly hadn't been fighting five minutes ago! He had kissed her as passionately as though he had meant it.

Dinner that evening made her doubt very much that he had. Brie had dressed in a simple cream silk cocktail dress, her hair swept up off her neck into a chignon for the evening, her throat adorned with a narrow gold chain. On her feet she wore light high-heeled mules. But the star of the evening was undoubtedly Helen Churchill, wearing dramatic scarlet, in a shimmering pant suit that Susan envied at once.

Why was she such a special guest? Brie wondered. There were only five guests, including Les whom she knew, and Helen, of course. The three other men were strangers, whom Adam introduced as members of his team. Brie thought that if Helen was there, Bill might have been an obvious dinner guest too, and therefore Claire...was a script-writer so much more important than the writer of the book that was being adapted? Brie didn't know, and didn't want to guess. It was bad enough to watch Helen going into action, charming all the men around Adam's table that evening, without speculating further, and she preferred to think that Bill and Claire may well have declined any dinner invitations at the moment, since they were on their honeymoon. And judging by Adam's impatience to get on with the work, a honeymoon that was going to be interrupted often enough.

Halfway through the meal, when Brie was tiring of listening to so much TV jargon she didn't understand, Helen's magnificent eyes were suddenly turned her way.

'How dull this must all be for you, Brie,' she said sweetly, knowing that it would be incomprehensible rather than dull, and implying that anyone excluded from the heady world of TV was a moron anyway. 'And how awful you must have felt with those silly reporters still linking you with Adam in that way in the garbage papers. We're all used to their lies to improve circulation, of course, but it must be galling for you.'

Brie felt her nerves prickle at the gushing attempt to put her down. 'Oh, I think I can cope,' she said evenly. 'It can be an occupational hazard, especially when you work in some of the titled households as I have. Being a children's nanny is considered to be fair game for some of the chinless wonders, but they soon learn their mistakes. And we come to the job well prepared for all the knocks, Helen. We're not made of cotton-wool, I promise you.'

She smiled back just as sweetly, and heard Adam give a low chuckle. So she had scored a point. It didn't thrill her. She felt angry at being obliged to answer Helen in the same bitchy way, knowing that neither was in any doubt of their dislike for the other. Brie hated herself for knowing darn well that in her case jealousy added to the barbs she made.

'Well, you won't be seeing too much of us,' Helen went on coolly. 'We'll be on location in the mountains most of the time, so you can get on with your little job with Susan.'

She turned away, leaving Brie fuming, and marvelling at her rudeness. But she didn't really care about Helen. And maybe her comment was all to the good. The less she saw of Adam the better, she thought feverishly, in one way at least. That kiss earlier on had proved to her just how vulnerable she was to him...she caught him looking at her over the rim of his crystal glass. He raised it slightly to her in silent acknowledgement, and his meaning was lost to her. She was only aware that Helen saw it too, and her eyes flashed in annoyance, while Brie's cheeks burned with embarrassment.

She had promised to stay, but she hoped desperately that being on location would keep Adam well out of her way, and that she could get on with the business of putting him out of her mind. The impossible sometimes happened...

## CHAPTER 11

In the next two weeks she hardly saw Adam at all. The T.V series was of major priority now, and if she missed him, then at least it was easier on her nerves when he wasn't around. Susan had settled into a mood nearer to apathy than contentment, and only came alive when she and Pottsy were racing along the water's edge at the beach, or fooling about together on the grass. Only with Pottsy did Susan seem like the child she really was, although she had stopped resenting Claire, to Brie's relief. Brie had given her a stern talking-to about that one morning.

'Susan, Claire's my friend, and I won't have you being rude to her. I want to see her often while she's here, and we could have a lot of fun together if you'd stop resenting her. It's up to you. We want to include you in our friendship, but we're not falling over backwards to do it. If you want to be treated like an adult, then just try behaving like one, all right?'

'You're supposed to be here for my benefit, not Claire's,' Susan sulked. 'After my rotten lessons, you're meant to keep me company.'

'So I shall, but you haven't always wanted me around, have you?' Brie asked bluntly. 'It's only now, when you feel threatened by Claire. And you needn't be, Susan. You must learn to accept that none of us has exclusive rights on another person.'

The thought swept through Brie's mind right then that if Adam Andrikos was hers, she would want exclusive rights on him, on his love, his name...she blinked, wondering if the fierceness of the thought had showed on her face right then. But already, Susan was turning away from her, burying her face in Pottsy's thick soft hair as she often did when she didn't want to show her feelings to anyone.

She was so transparent, Brie thought then, with the quick rush of affection she couldn't help feeling for Susan, despite all her tantrums. As though showing love was a sign of weakness in Susan's eyes...was that one more thing her strong-willed father had instilled in her? Brie wondered.

'O.K Claire's not so bad, anyway,' Susan said carelessly.

And Brie had to be content with that. But at least the times when Claire joined them at the beach or the villa passed more comfortably. Except that Brie should have known that her friend would sense the turbulence of Brie's emotions. They had known each other too long for Brie to hide it from her for ever.

'Why don't you tell me what's wrong, Brie?' Claire said one afternoon, when Susan and Pottsy were screaming in the rolling waves together, and she and Brie were sunbathing, the golden tan of Brie's skin deepening to a glorious honey colour, Claire's still in the early stages. 'You've got dark shadows under your eyes, and a look of strain around your mouth. Aren't you sleeping? Does the little brat drive you so crazy?' She finished with an affectionate grin.

Brie seized on her words, 'I don't sleep very well,' she said. 'I can't get used to the climate, I guess, and if I close all my windows and turn on the air-conditioning, I feel claustrophobic. That's all. I'll get used to it in time, I suppose.'

'You should be used to it by now,'

Claire said bluntly. 'Is that all it is? The gorgeous Adam's not been giving you a hard time?'

'Nope. He's too busy with his series and the equally gorgeous Helen. I told you a long time ago not to go linking us together. It still applies, Claire.'

'Does it?' Claire's eyes searched Brie's. She shook her head slowly. 'What a shame. You two are so obviously made for each other.'

Brie gave a short laugh, settling back on the soft sand, and feeling its warmth caress her shoulders. As warm as Adam's touch...she shook off the longing.

'Now you're falling into the journalist's trap, darling,' she said lightly. 'It all makes good copy, but that's all. Life's not made up of neat little compartments, is it? You and Bill just happened to be lucky, that's all.'

Claire lay down again, a blissful smile curving her mouth.

'We certainly did,' she agreed.

Brie closed her eyes against the brightness of the sun and sea. Even when he wasn't around, she was burningly aware of his presence. This was Adam's beach, his patch of land, his home. She slept in a room that belonged to him, that reflected his tastes; she drank his wine and ate at his table. She admired his paintings and his choice of books. She breathed the air that he breathed, touched the ground he trod. Ye gods, she thought prosaically as her thoughts raced on, she was in danger of becoming besotted by the whole concept of the man...she counted the days until her time here would be over. Counted them with longing and dread, knowing it would be an episode in her life that was finished. Yet knowing that while she breathed, the love she felt for Adam would never be over. She had never experienced love like this before, so pulsatingly alive that it seemed to take over her entire being. It scared her...

The tranquility of that lovely afternoon was abruptly shattered. Brie's own thoughts froze in her head as she heard the piercing scream. She jerked her head up from the sand, spinning round so fast she felt dizzy. Claire too...

'What on earth was that?' Claire gasped, leaping to her feet.

Brie grabbed up her sun top and hauled it over her swimsuit, filled with a sudden fear. Susan had been screaming with delight just a short while ago, racing in the surf with Pottsy. They were nowhere to be seen now, and that scream had been far from joyful. She raced over the sand, her bare feet seeming to get nowhere, Claire right behind her. She reached the lane just as Susan came rushing down to fetch her. Susan, her mobile little face working in agony, the tears streaming down her face. Brie just had time to register the fact when Susan hurled herself into Brie's arms.

'Oh, come quick! Pottsy's been run over. I think—I think he's dead! Come quick, Brie. I can't look—I can't—'

The sobs spilled over. Her fingers dug into Brie's bare arms like needles. Brie could feel the shocked tremors in every inch of Susan's body. She grabbed her hand at once and raced back with her the way Susan had come, praying with every bit of her strength that the dog wasn't dead...

Susan's breath was a ragged gasping by the time they reached the road. Through the sobs, Brie managed to get a garbled story about Pottsy breaking free to chase something that had caught his attention, and had gone right into the path of the tourist's hire car.

'He didn't even stop!' Susan wept hysterically. 'He didn't care—'

Brie aimed a careful slap, hard on the side of Susan's cheek. The red weal showed up at once, but it barely stopped the flow of tears. All this time, Brie had wanted her to cry, to show some emotion, and now it seemed ironic that she tried to stop it, she thought wryly. She looked quietly at the prone figure of the dog, pathetically silent, and knelt down beside him, since Susan seemed suddenly incapable of movement.

'Susan, he's not dead,' Brie said at once. 'Listen to me, will you? Pottsy's not dead. I can feel him breathing. Put your head against his side gently, and you'll feel it too—'

The girl scrambled to do as Brie said, shivering uncontrollably. Claire had joined them now, loaded up with all the beach gear. Her eyes met Brie's. It was true that Pottsy wasn't dead, but to her it seemed that his breathing was very shallow. She was no expert on animal injuries, and she spoke quickly to Claire.

'Would you go to the villa and ask Miguel or Stavros to come with the car to take Pottsy to a vet? They must know of one on the island. I'll stay here with Susan.'

Just in case the breathing stopped, she added silently. Though that was a prospect she didn't dare to imagine. Susan's nerves were so finely tuned already, she couldn't guess on the effect her dog's demise might have on her. Brie took comfort in the fact that as Susan spoke in a choking, soothing voice to him, Pottsy's tail tried a very feeble wag in response, and his tongue managed a dry little lick at her hand.

Claire didn't take long to reach the villa and deliver the message, Brie thought in thankfulness as she heard one of the Andrikos cars pull up alongside them. Then her heart stopped momentarily before it raced on, as Adam got out of it swiftly.

'I just got back from location,' he said rapidly, kneeling down by Pottsy at once. Susan turned into his arms, flinging herself at him, tears flooding her face again.

'Oh Adam, say he's not going to die. He's all I've got. You won't let him die, will you?'

'Hey, hold on,' Adam said roughly as she clung to him. 'You don't think this little guy's going to die from a bump on the head, do you? He'll be fine, sweetheart—'

'How do you know?' Susan sobbed. 'They said Mummy was going to be fine, and she died. Daddy told me so, and then they both died. Why should I believe you? I don't want to lose Pottsy, I don't! I love him, and he loves me—'

'I love you too, Susan.' Adam suddenly folded her to his chest in a fiercely protective movement. 'Pottsy's not going to die, but even if he did, you'd still have me. You're not all alone in the world, you little idiot!'

Brie wondered if it was the first time in his life he'd told Susan she meant anything to him. She guessed instinctively that it was, both from the embarrassed way the words were wrenched from him, and the stunned look on Susan's face. But right now she was too concerned with Pottsy's fate to explore the incredulous possibility that Adam actually loved her. She gave a shuddering breath and asked quickly if they should take Pottsy to the vet or take him back to the villa at once.

'Neither,' Adam said more briskly. 'Claire's passing on the message to Juanita and she's calling the vet to come out here.

I didn't want to risk moving him until we see the damage, but I don't imagine it's too serious by the looks of him.'

Brie looked down, and saw to her relief that Pottsy seemed to be recovering. He whimpered now and then, but he tried to lick Susan's hand again as though to reassure her, and from the way his breathing had regulated, and he didn't appear too distressed, Brie guessed that no bones were broken. And if Adam and Susan were at last to lose their inhibitions and talk about the past, sharing grief and love, then that would be the second miracle that day.

Brie wouldn't count on it though. Nor did she stop to consider that her own feelings hardly mattered any more. She was too concerned with the little trio here, almost oblivious to her presence, and right now she wouldn't have had it any other way.

It was blisteringly hot waiting by the roadside for the vet's car to appear. The earth was dry and dusty, and tiny lizards lay motionless, basking in the sun, or scuttled for a sliver of shade. At long last a vehicle careered round the same corner the tourist had taken too fast, and came to a stop beside them.

Adam gave him the details in a concise manner, and the vet knelt beside Pottsy, his fingers feeling gently for signs of broken bones and bleeding. He said cheerfully that there seemed to be none.

'I'd like to take him back to the surgery to give him a good going over though. You did well not to move him, but my guess is he just got knocked out for a few minutes, didn't you, old fellow?'

He ruffled Pottsy's ears, and the dog gave a growl of pleasure.

'Can I come?' Susan said at once. 'Can I stay with him? You won't keep him all night, will you?'

Her voice held fear, and Brie guessed it was the same fear that had gripped her when her parents were taken to hospital. She wasn't fully aware of all the details, but it wasn't hard to piece together.

'Of course you can come,' the vet said freely. 'And if Mr Andrikos wants to follow in his car, I dare say you'll be able to take the dog home in an hour or so.'

Susan's tears were disappearing fast. The vulnerability was soon hidden beneath its habitual mask. Adam, too, looked relieved but a little impatient. Was the TV work so all-important that he couldn't spare the time to go with Susan? Brie thought in a burst of outrage.

'Can't you do this for her?' Brie exploded, once the vet had taken Pottsy and Susan off with him. 'Is it too much to ask that you unbend and show some compassion? This must be the first time she's cried since her parents died, Adam. Can't you see that she needed this? That she needs *you?* Can't you love her for more than a minute of your precious time?'

'Is the lecture over? If so, I suggest you let me go and get the car,' he said coldly. 'I thought I'd told her I loved her, so what more do you want of me?'

'You told her, but you didn't *show* it for more than a minute!' Brie said passionately. 'Let her know that you care, Adam, before it's too late. Tell her the words, but show it in the way you act with her. She's growing into a woman and she's hurt and bewildered by the past six months. Stop treating her like a child—'

He looked at her oddly for a moment as the words choked in her throat. Poor little rich girl, Brie couldn't help thinking, and here she was, trying to tell this implacable, successful man how to run his life...he turned on his heel and strode away from her back to the villa. Brie stared after him, feeling all the passion drain out of her. What had she achieved, except to alienate him still further from her? She felt a sense of failure such as she never had before. She wanted so much to help Susan...she wanted so much for Adam to fold his arms around her own shoulders and tell her he agreed with everything. She wanted him to love her...

Brie brushed away the angry sting of tears, berating herself for being a hopeless, romantic fool, thinking she could change the world—at least, the small part of it that was Adam Andrikos's world. Why should he take notice of Brie's opinions? She was nothing to him, while he was, and always would be, everything to her. The sweet bitter pain of it caught at her throat as she walked back to the villa herself, trying to compose herself before seeing Claire again.

'Thank goodness Pottsy's all right. At least, Adam thought he was.' Claire searched Brie's flushed face with puzzled eyes. 'He wasn't just kidding me, was he, Brie? The dog's going to be O.K, isn't he? Nothing's broken?'

For a few seconds Brie couldn't speak, and when she did the words came out thick.

'Nothing's broken,' she said. Only her heart, and her spirit was in danger of cracking up too. 'He'll be all right as far as I know, Claire.'

'Thank goodness. Susan looked shattered, and you don't look too good either—'

To Brie's relief, Bill arrived to collect Claire at that moment, and her friend didn't pursue the question of just why Brie looked so dejected. As the newlyweds drove away, Brie felt a sharp twist of envy for their happiness, and wondered bleakly if it was a happiness that would forever elude her. Bill had spoken briefly of prelims and shootings and stunt shots, already into the TV jargon, yet once he and Claire had sat together in the car, the smile Bill had given his wife excluded everything else from his mind. It was at once beautiful and poignant for Brie to see it. And she had the temerity to think that Adam Andrikos could ever feel that way about *her!* He was too immersed in his work to care about anything else, she told herself bitterly, even Susan.

She was sipping a cool glass of wine when she heard Adam's car arrive back at the villa, feeling the need of it to relax her. Pottsy bounded in first, tail wagging furiously as he licked Brie's hand, and obviously quite recovered. Susan was hardly less exuberant, her eyes shining like stars, and with everything about her more buoyant that Brie had even seen it before.

'Adam's fixed it for me to go to school in Athens next term,' she burst out. 'We're flying over in his plane tomorrow to see the headmaster. Isn't it fantastic? He says we'll be able to see more of each other, and I can come home weekends—'

She positively glowed, and Adam had a smug smile on his face. The two of them looked so different, somehow, so much a family all of a sudden, that although she had brought all this about, Brie felt ridiculously left out and a little hurt that Adam was getting all the credit. Susan hugged his arm, and he seemed to like it. And from then on, all the talk that evening was of the new school and how clever Adam had been to fix it, and what a wonderful surprise he had given her, and she was going to be good from now on...

Brie had a genuine headache by the time she said she was going to bed early as she had some letters to write. Adam moved swiftly to open the door for her. Just as though she was a visitor, she thought miserably. He put his hand on her arm, and she felt as though its warmth branded her.

'Thank you, Brie,' he said quietly. 'We had a good talk while we waited for the vet's verdict on Pottsy. We talked about our parents, and the future, and everything from cabbages to kings.'

'I'm glad.' Brie said in a muffled voice. 'That's what I meant by showing love. It's not hard once you get the hang of it.'

She got out of the room as fast as she could, away from the nearness of him that played havoc with her nerves and turned her emotions upside down. Away from those dark eyes that seemed to see inside her soul, and yet couldn't see the love she felt for him. Or didn't want to see it, which was more like it. She was nothing important in his life, except that she'd been a tiny catalyst in making him aware of Susan's needs. Brie's own needs were something else. She leaned against the door in her own room, fighting back the tears. Should she get away from here tomorrow, while the two of them were in Athens? It would be an ideal opportunity. She could phone the airport, take the first available plane, get back to London and fly right on to Scotland to her parents' home. It had been a haven before, and could be again...

Even as she thought it, Brie knew it wasn't the answer. And she wasn't in the habit of running out on a job. She was realistic enough to know that Susan's high could as quickly come tumbling down, and then Brie would be needed. Just as she would be needed when Adam went off on location. She was happily surprised that he was taking tomorrow off without a second thought.

Unless all this had already been planned. It could have been, but Brie thought not. Adam knew enough influential people to go where he liked, any time he liked. The fact just widened the gulf between their two lives.

Susan was still elated the next morning. Right after breakfast she and Adam drove off to the tiny airstrip, and later, Brie saw the small private plane circle over the villa before heading towards the Greek mainland and Athens. The day was hers to do as she wanted, yet she couldn't settle to anything. Claire had taken the day to go on location with Bill, at his invitation, and the day dragged for Brie. Meals came and went and she couldn't have said what she ate, and was annoyed with herself for being so feeble.

But this day was important, to Susan and to Adam. She hoped that it would forge something special in their relationship, and tried to ignore that gnawing feeling of being so much the outsider after all.

She heard the drone of the small private plane around six-thirty that evening. She was trying to read a magazine on the patio, and although her heartbeats quickened, she deliberately refrained from looking into the sky. It was only when the plane seemed to lose height and circled the villa several times, that Brie shielded her eyes against the brightness of the sun, squinting skywards. Yes, it was Adam's plane...

Her heart suddenly leapt. Trailing from the plane was a streamer with a message written on it in huge letters for all the island to see. But the words were obviously intended for one person only.

'I love you, angel. Will you marry me?'

Brie read tremulously.

She didn't remember getting up from the patio chair or waving her hand. She saw the plane's wings dip in a small salute, then it circled the villa once more before moving off in the direction of the airstrip. And then, as the sound died away, and she was conscious only of the beat of her own heart, Brie wondered if it had really happened or if she had imagined it. Had she wanted it so much, that she had conjured up such a fantasy? She felt dazed, and totally disorientated.

One thing was certain. Suddenly struck by a burst of ridiculous shyness, Brie knew she couldn't simply sit here on the patio inanely and wait for Adam to drive to the villa. Especially with Susan there, who would by now be bubbling over with news of her day. She would be excited over Adam's ingenious message too. Let her tell it all to Juanita first, Brie thought shakily. She had to see Adam alone, to know if she was dreaming, or if the streamer message was unbelievably, gloriously real...

She went quickly to her room, hot and clammy, and needing something to do to fill the time until Adam would be here. It would be at least half an hour...she peeled off her sundress and went into her shower room, to stand beneath the warm soft water and let the tumbling thoughts race over themselves in her mind.

Adam loved her. Adam wanted to marry her. The joy of it was like an intense wave of pleasure rushing over her each time the message soared into her senses. Was this a side effect of all Brie had tried to tell him on Susan's account? she wondered. Say the words, but show the love. And Adam had shown the words...

Brie patted her skin dry with trembling hands, then tied a towelling robe around her body. She felt too agitated even to dress yet, and there was plenty of time. She would wait for Adam in his sanctuary, his study, where not even Susan went unless she was invited, or commanded. She would wait for him there...

She lay on the bed for a few moments, staring at the ceiling, still aware of the drumbeats of her heart. Trying to breathe slowly, to still them a little, but it was difficult, because every few seconds his words leapt into her mind, stimulating all her senses.

'I love you, angel. Will you marry me?'

She closed her eyes with the sheer joy

of it. It couldn't have been a fantasy, or a publicity stunt, she thought agonisingly. Adam couldn't be that cruel...if he was, then she wouldn't have the strength to bear it. She would retreat into that strange half-world that Susan had recently inhabited, closing her mind to pains and joys and love...

Brie moved restlessly. As she did so, she became aware of a new pressure on her bed. She had blotted out the unwelcome picture of rejected love, and must have slipped into a brief sleep.

Now, as her eyes opened dreamily, she looked right into Adam's face. His dear, beloved face, the darkly penetrating eyes searching hers. He had obviously come right up here as soon as he arrived at the villa. He wore the cool cotton shirt of the morning, and the elegant yet casual slacks. He smelled a faintly raw masculine smell that mingled erotically with Brie's liberally splashed-on body lotion. He leaned over her, his hands warm on her shoulders through the towelling robe, his breath a soft caress as his sensual mouth formed the words Brie had so ached to hear.

'I hope my message was plain enough, darling. Show my love, you said, didn't you? I thought about that over and over, and it finally broke through my addled brain that you were the one I wanted to show it to the most. Why else would I have insisted you keep to your appointment here, when anyone else would have been sent packing weeks ago for talking to me the way you do? Why else would I find it almost impossible to keep my hands off you, let alone my eyes? Why else would I be asking you to marry me, angel?'

Brie's voice came slowly, low and thick.

'Is that what you're asking me, Adam? I didn't dream it?'

Even now, she couldn't quite believe it. Even now, when his hands were circling her shoulders in small spirals, edging the robe away from her soft skin, and pressing his mouth to its damp fresh texture. Even now, she had to make him say it again, and again...

'I'm asking, and I'm waiting for an answer, woman,' he growled in mock impatience. 'And since you're so insistent on being shown what's too important to be believed by mere words, I also intend putting my words into action.'

'Do you?' Brie whispered, as his mouth hovered a breath above hers. 'After all this time of putting me in my place as Susan's keeper—'

'Forget about Susan,' he said seductively. 'She's up on her own cloud now. Let's get back to ours.'

Brie moved away from him, which only had the effect of giving him more room to slide on the bed beside her. Her heart pounded, but she had to be sure. She wasn't cut out to be part of some publicity stunt, and she was too much in love with Adam to play around. It was difficult to concentrate when his hands and mouth were doing such delicious things to her, and electrifying her skin wherever they touched.

'Isn't this all a bit sudden?' Brie asked faintly, as his fingers moved to the tie of her robe and she felt the freedom of the air caress her midriff before Adam's lips warmed it with a kiss. She felt his palm slide gently upwards, cupping the underside of her breast before he claimed it possessively.

'Why the inquisition, darling? I want you to marry me. Can I make it any plainer than that? And if you've ever bothered to read any of those hack journalists' profiles on me, then among all the fantasy they dream up, you might have noticed that they always give me credit for saying exactly what I think. And what's sudden about it anyway? Didn't I offer once before to make an honest woman of you?' he demanded, still tracing patterns over her suntanned skin and making her shiver with barely suppressed excitement.

'I didn't know I was meant to take that seriously,' Brie began to laugh, and then the laughter died in her eyes, because more than anything in her life before, this was serious. This was real, and the ache inside her was fast becoming an overpowering longing to belong to Adam totally. She ran the tip of her tongue around her suddenly dry lips. She made a swift movement so that she was half sitting up, her long silken hair trailing into his face as he gazed up at her. Oblivious of the fact that she was half naked, her eyes burned into his, demanding the truth.

'Adam, I'm not one of your sophisticated glamour girls, nor a brilliant script-writer, nor anything like the kind of woman you must meet every day.' Her voice was wobbly and scratchy, and she hated herself for humbling herself, but she had to make things very clear to him or there was no future for them. They had to be honest with each other.

'I care nothing for that,' Adam answered in a low throb of sound. 'Don't you know that to me you're the most beautiful, sexy, desirable woman on earth? Don't you know that love makes stars of us all? And I love you, Brie. God, how I love you!'

He pulled her down on him, enveloping her in his arms, and sliding his hands inside the towelling robe to caress the tenseness of her spine. His hands slid upwards, moving through her hair, enfolding her to him. His needs were blatantly obvious to her, and desire sang in her veins like a symphony.

'You said, "I love you, angel",' she mumbled against the rough texture of his cheek. Through the thin cotton of his shirt she could feel the rapid beat of his heart, the hard firm breadth of his chest. The flat male nipples were as taut as her own. The awareness of it seemed to fill her with strange new sensations, as though her limbs were flowing with molten honey, warm and sensual. 'Why those words, Adam?'

His hands moved down the length of her

spine until they captured the neat curves of her rear, squeezing and caressing.

'Why? Because I knew damn well that everyone who saw them would recognise them, that's why! So the whole world would know that Adam Andrikos was asking his angel to marry him,' he said with a touch of his professional flamboyance. He gripped her waist now. She could hardly breathe. 'So when are you going to say yes, angel? Or do I have to stay here all night before I get the answer I want? I can promise you, I'm quite prepared to. In fact, I can think of nothing more pleasurable.' His voice dropped to a sexy burr, his meaning quite clear.

Brie gave a small giggle, her spirits suddenly soaring. She still couldn't resist teasing him a little more.

'And outrage Juanita and your sister—'

'To blazes with them,' Adam growled back, directing her fingers to the buttons on his shirt, which Brie tried not to unfasten with indecent haste. She leaned forward against him when they were all undone, feeling the sweet sharp pleasure of her flesh against his, his warmth embracing her warmth, two sets of heartbeats as one. The silken fall of her hair made a golden curtain between them as she lay her mouth against his.

'Aren't you hungry, Adam?' she murmured, knowing that Juanita would be preparing dinner at this very moment.

'Very,' he said. 'But not for food!'

He shook her gently as the bubbling laughter filled her throat once more. The arrogant male in him was demanding her submission now, and he quickly reversed their positions, so that Brie lay laughing up at him, her eyes sparkling like diamonds, her parted mouth softly jewelled, waiting...

'Am I wasting my time on you, Brie?' he said softly. 'If I am, just say so. If you don't love me already, then I'll just have to spend a little longer teaching you. If it takes the rest of our lives, angel, I promise I'll teach you to love me—'

The time for laughter, for flippancy, was over. Brie's hands went to his face, the Greek god features that she loved so much, and she held it fiercely, wanting him as urgently as he wanted her.

'I do love you, Adam. I love you so much it almost frightens me. And I'll marry you—tomorrow—next week—just as soon as possible—'

She couldn't say more, because he was

smothering her with kisses, and leaving her in no doubt of the strength of his feelings. Time and space ceased to have meaning for either of them from that moment on, as Adam made love to her, his body taking possession of hers with infinite gentleness, until her senses were aroused to the peak of perfection. She knew at last the wonder of love, the completeness of love, and the miracle of it was that this was only the beginning. The prelude to the continuing love story that was Adam and Brie.

**Other MAGNA Romance Titles In Large Print**

ROSE BOUCHERON
The Massinghams

VIRGINIA COFFMAN
The Royles

RUTH HAMILTON
Nest Of Sorrows

SHEILA JANSEN
Mary Maddison

NANCY LIVINGSTON
Never Were Such Times

GENEVIEVE LYONS
The Palucci Vendetta

MARY MINTON
Every Street

## Other MAGNA Romance Titles In Large Print

CATRIN MORGAN
Comfort Me With Apples

JEAN SAUNDERS
All In The April Morning

JUDITH SAXTON
Nobody's Children

HELEN UPSHALL
A House Full of Women

ANNE VIVIS
Daughters Of Strathannan

DEE WILLIAMS
Carrie Of Culver Road

MARY WILLIAMS
Castle Carnack

**Other MAGNA Romance Titles In Large Print**

MARGARET BARKER
Surgeon Royal

MARY BOWRING
Vet In Charge

FRANCES CROWNE
Dangerous Symptoms

ANGELA DEVINE
Crock Of Gold

HOLLY NORTH
Nurse At Large

ANNA RAMSAY
The Legend Of Dr Markland

JUDITH WORTHY
Locum Lover